wild
mulberries

wild
mulberries

Iman Humaydan Younes

Translated by
Michelle Hartman

ARABIA BOOKS
LONDON

This edition published in the United Kingdom in 2010 by

ARABIA BOOKS Ltd
70 Cadogan Place, London SW1X 9AH
www.arabia-books.com

Copyright © by Iman Humaydan Younes 2008
Translation copyright © by Michelle Hartman 2008

Published in the USA by Interlink Books
an imprint of Interlink Publishing Group, Inc.

ISBN 978-1-906697-27-3

Printed in Great Britain by
CPI William Clowes, Suffolk NR34 7TL

A CIP catalogue for this book is available from the British Library

To my father

1

Nothing... Nothing is like a small warm drop of water sliding down the back of my neck. A small sting that elicits a sudden "ah" from within me. A sleeping "ah" that I reckoned was born already advanced in years. A drop of water shines on a little almond leaf... The drops cluster together, becoming round then flowing toward the ground. A warm drop of water falls and melts slowly, drawing a moist, zigzagging line on my skin, which warms my body, despite how cold it is. I open my eyes again and a feeble sun is shining above me. I get up on cold, stiff toes and stand in order to shake off the moist dust.

I do not know how long I slept here. I may have slumbered for hours. I leave the valley at the bottom of the village and climb up toward the house. This valley is the safest place—it has no cliff or chasm beyond it. It is the very lowest point. Lower than all other points around it. It is almost exactly at sea level. My cold damp feet sink into the moist muddy soil and as I climb up to the higher path, my body feels increasingly heavy, as though my feet are bound to the earth. "This is where the princess of wild plants lives." I remember my friend Doha's words as I pass the abandoned stone vaulted room encircled by medlar and cypress trees. She would say that to me every time we went down into the lowest part of the valley. I reach the foot of the incline where the path ends. I take a deep breath and then I race off, shouting "ahhh.... ahhh..." I scream while running on the damp, colorful carpet that first emerges at the beginning of March, sprouting up to cover the land. I am free, like smooth, hot, gushing water, like a prisoner passing through the prison gate to enter the outside world. My voice echoes back from the depths of the valley. I run—then I run some more. I cross the fresh green field and reach the narrow dirt path that goes up toward the *haara*. I continue. Then I pause to catch my breath. Panting, I look back, but I see nothing but the road stretched out behind me like the tail of a snake.

I arrive at the *haara* and at our house. The house that has no women, yet is full of them; where many women have come and gone. My father is a man who has passed the age of sixty and has no woman—and yet he has all the women. When night falls, only my paternal aunt and I remain. The echo of our voices and the sounds of dinnertime pots and pans reverberate within the walls that separate the house into parts and connect to a spacious courtyard onto which the doors of the *haara* open. Windows in the walls surrounding the square courtyard rise high above it like the windows of a prison. At the end of the night, my father's footsteps can be heard approaching the outer gate.

A black iron gate that rises austerely near an ancient walnut tree, to reach a ceiling built out of an enormous yellow boulder. He approaches the courtyard while continuing to tap the end of his walking stick on the ground. My aunt wakes up and, just as she does every night, turns automatically and half asleep to open the inner gate of the *haara* for him. He enters without a word. Only the clicks of his walking stick and his footsteps echo inside the walls. Around dawn my half-brother returns to the *haara*. Sometimes he is gone for many nights and then appears once again. The men of this house don't like to spend their evenings in it. They go out and do not come back. My aunt doesn't usually leave the light in the *haara* on for them. She has left a lantern on in only one room and it throws a weak light on the long *liwan* while we sleep. I toss and turn and do not fall asleep. When I finally do drift off in the dawn hours, my mother appears to me in a dream, with the same face and the same clothes as in the picture. This is the only picture the people of the *haara* forgot, on the corner table in the locked salon. She left home when I not yet three years old. I have forgotten everything about her. I've built a memory of her from fragments of conversations I've heard between my aunt and our female relatives and neighbors. What she was like and how she disappeared. Twelve years have passed and there is still gossip; it's only increased now that I have come of age. And my aunt has realized it.

2

It is an oppressive morning... The sun rose late. Spring fog lifting from the outstretched coastline wraps itself around the *haara*. The blooming flowers growing on the door of my room, which leads outside to the courtyard, are a conspicuous yellow. The fog screens them from the bright sunlight; it seems as though it is behind translucent glass. My aunt weakly mumbles something I can't understand. A familiar scent penetrates the door to reach my nose. I go out barefoot to the washstand and see my aunt circling the large tray used for roasting coffee beans around and around over the burning embers in the winter room. The fragrant, deeply scented vapors fill the women circled around stove with pleasure.

Muti'a is singing. She is the Circassian woman who came from Aleppo and rented a room for herself and her husband in the upper *haara*. That was the first time that my father had rented a room to strangers. She has been here for fourteen years, so she knew my mother. Her voice lifts up slowly, incrementally, and when she reaches the "Ah" it gets weaker and becomes more melancholy. She also sings in her spacious room, which she divided into two using a wardrobe, other furniture and a cotton curtain. Out of one big living space, she created two rooms: one for sleeping and the other for receiving guests. She kept one sunny corner near the window for cooking and washing. My aunt enjoys Muti'a's singing and encourages her, though she is afraid, in the presence of my father, to lift her own voice in song or even to join Muti'a. But perhaps she is not as afraid of her brother the shaykh as much as she is of her own voice. She may be afraid that her voice will come rushing out from deep inside her and rise until she will somehow no longer be able to control it—like an untamed animal escaped from its cage, burning with desire and completely wild. Doesn't Muti'a say that a woman's desires are like sleeping tigers: once awakened, no one will ever again be able to curb them.

"Sing, Shams... Sing..." Muti'a says.

My aunt begins singing shyly, but her voice is thick, deep, unreliable, and festering as though it were dying. She stops in the middle of the song and then starts up again. Meanwhile Muti'a stretches out the leg folded underneath her and massages it with her right hand. She raises her left hand above her head and accompanies my aunt's voice with rhythmic beats while a mix of hidden pain and joy shifts between her eyes and lips.

I learned the history of the house from my brother. My half-brother on my father's side. My father's first wife only bore one son. My brother is truly more of a father to me. When I address him, I add the word "brother" to his name. Many years stand between me and my father, who moved to the *haaras* with his sister, my aunt, when he married my mother. She was the only daughter of my grandfather, who came from Argentina to search for his roots. My grandfather's large family all left the village during the events of 1860. No family members remained except Ibrahim, who was only related distantly, by marriage. My grandfather had intended to return to Argentina and continue his business manufacturing medicines, for tropical diseases we had never even heard of, made from wild herbs and grasses. But then the First World War broke out and he was forced to stay in the village. Its inhabitants soon got used to seeking his advice on every health problem they encountered. They also got used to calling him "Doctor." My grandfather bought the *haaras* and the fields in the valley, which—with Ibrahim's help—he began cultivating with strange plants, whose seeds he had brought with him from Argentina. He had a bony, slender frame, and never befriended anyone but my father, who protected him and introduced him to the people of the village. My father had no trouble at all integrating my grandfather into his group of friends—the village's young men and "*qabadays*." This was easy for him, despite the fact that my grandfather did not enjoy even one characteristic that would qualify him to be called a *qabaday*. My grandfather was perhaps the only man who was never defeated, even with his fragile build. Perhaps the leanness and gentleness of his body kept him protected. Physical weakness accompanied by inner strength and knowledge was a rare combination among the men of the village. My grandfather died only two months after I was born. My brother stayed with his mother, whom my father had divorced. He did not return to the *haara* until after my mother had disappeared.

My aunt did not change after her brother married my mother, despite moving from the small house to the *haara*. The green marble tiles, the huge chandeliers hanging from the ceiling, and the honey-colored velvet armchairs scattered throughout the middle *haara* and its rooms didn't change my aunt's way of living. She slept on the ground even though she was surrounded by many bedrooms with brass beds. They did not remain merely bedrooms. She transformed them into sitting rooms and sometimes rooms for eating, and she also used the wardrobes within their thick walls for storing provisions, woolen bed covers and rugs. And for two months every year, the *haara*s were also transformed into a workshop for raising silkworms.

Our way of living has changed little from how it was before my mother left. The woman who takes care of me, that is to say my aunt, keeps sewing me dresses out of the old clothes given to her by English women, and fashions long shirts for herself out of flour sacks made of raw linen.

ﷺ

One large room remains empty throughout the year. This room is at the front of the long *liwan*, whose green marble floor shines, its tiles reflecting the light bursting through the large door that opens onto the courtyard and the upper *haara* on the east and on the west leads to the spacious *dawwara* that is cultivated with mulberry, lemon, loquat and fig trees.

In this room alone, no one ever sleeps or sits. Its first door opens onto the large *liwan*, which has two brass chandeliers hanging from its high ceiling, their long candlesticks filled with ivory-colored candles. My aunt has never lit them—not once. This room has sofas of different sizes and colors, their fabric embroidered in dark green, pistachio, and yellow. The round pillows are edged with threadbare beige tassels. The room seems like a repository for furniture that no one ever uses, each piece a perfect companion to the others. A round wooden table is placed in one of its corners and its ancient, cracked surface is covered with a filigreed white cloth. Silver frames containing black-and-white pictures are lined up on this table. A large portrait of my father hangs on the eastern wall above the divan, which were it not for its cushions would have seemed like a narrow, elevated bed. No doubt my father the shaykh prepared himself carefully for the portrait so that he would appear in it exactly as he always dreamed to be—in his *'uqqal* and *kuffiyah*, colored *sitra* and flowing *sirwal*.

He still keeps these clothes in his wardrobe, just as he still hangs his gun and sword on his bedroom wall. As for his moustache, it remains as it is in the portrait, though it is a little thinner now and has turned white.

My father reports that he wore those clothes for the last time during the revolution against the French more than ten years ago and that he lost a lot of blood and would have died had it not been for one of the revolutionaries, who carried him on his horse, walking with them all the way to the village of Soueida in Jabal al-Druze. The truth that the shaykh does not mention is that he wasn't participating in the revolution. Rather he found himself in the middle of a battle while on a business trip; at that time he was smuggling guns inside jerry cans of oil with double bottoms, then with the profit he made off the guns, he bought large sacks of wheat and returned to Lebanon to sell them. Most of the pictures on the table are of friends and relatives, none of whom I know. I cannot find a picture of me, or of my aunt, or even a picture of my brother. There is a small picture of an English woman and man; they are Mrs. and Mr. Porter and my mother sits between them, my grandfather stands behind. The picture is very small compared to the others. It is placed on the edge of the table in an inconspicuous place, always behind bigger, taller pictures. Despite this, I can still clearly discern where the picture was taken—the *dawwara* courtyard behind the middle *haara*. Behind my young mother, I see the loquat tree, which looks much smaller than it is now. My grandfather's body covers a part of the edge of the round fountain in the middle of the courtyard, which is still filled many times a day so that the animals can drink from it and the fish that my aunt raises can live in it. I pass my hand up and down over the cold glass that encloses the picture of my mother, grandfather, and the English couple. My aunt's voice from the depths of the *liwan* wakes me from the languorous daydreaming that I love and prefer to enjoy alone. Her voice is like a hurricane striking the walls of the *haara*, entering into its stone pores, penetrating glass, iron, and my bones. Her voice injures me. I retreat from the room and start running toward the wide main gate, the one that encloses the two *haara*s and opens out only onto the house's inner courtyard. From there, the scents of jasmine and basil rise and mingle with the warm cooking smells coming from the depths of Muti'a's room. I scramble up into the big walnut tree, which rises into space, its long branches reaching out into the sky of the courtyard, like a fresh green net, through which the rays of the sun and the colors of the day pass. I climb up the iron gate toward the stone roof. I pause and then continue my ascent toward the branches of the walnut tree that are spread out above me. Below me, I see the jasmine that has grown and spread over the wall of the high *haara,* covering it completely. I see the blooming roses that my aunt decorates with eggshells to protect them from the evil eye and around whose stems she ties colored ribbons that she brings from the shrines of Sayyid Abdullah and Sitt Sha'awana and Nabi Ayyoub. I reach the highest branch and stay there for long hours, flying in a wide-open space, suspended between heaven and earth.

I almost remember my mother's face. Its contours flash through my mind; often I can just about make out its precise features. In my imagination, it constantly changes between golden brown and shining, translucent white. Certain confident moments about this face flash through me, dissipate, and are gone. Except for a faint smell that touches me whenever I try to remember my mother. A perfumed scent emanated from her skin, which she never put anything on but soap and water. Isn't this what my father always says? That her skin emitted a sweet perfume instead of sweat? My mother is a woman of the unknown. I did not know the woman in her just as I never knew the mother. She is neither a woman nor a mother. I reincarnate her picture; it reveals nothing to me except an apparition with no substance or body. I try to collect small shards of news about her just as a mason binds together bricks and mud to rebuild a house struck by an earthquake. In the end, however, I have nothing concrete, only fragments of memory that I try to construct without success.

This tortures me. What tortures me are moments that I remember and I do not know if they really exist or are images from the memories of the people around me, which I have collected like a beggar to create a memory all my own. I have grown used to the many, constant questions of my aunt's guests, "Have you heard anything about her?"

I know that they are asking about my mother. She has lost her name here. She no longer has a name; she has become merely a grammatical ending. A pronoun in the feminine form.

"Vanished into thin air," my father repeats, "As they say, when you put a grain of salt in water, it dissolves and is gone."

"The goat that eats acorns cannot digest them and dies," my aunt comments, hardly concealing her scorn. She means that a person who lives a different life will never be accepted there nor will she ever be able to return. Then she lets out a long echoing sigh, "akh... akh ..." It is as though she wants to say that she is different from my mother, who is now paying the price for her sins, and that she will not be saved from her punishment just because she is far from here.

"You shut up!" he says to her angrily. She does not shut up, but continues, "I knew from the beginning that this would happen!"

"What do you know? Say it! You don't know anything!" my father scolds her again. This time my aunt keeps quiet. She knows the skaykh is really angry and means what he says, that is, she should be quiet. My aunt knows this and I'm guessing that every time my aunt brings up my mother's life story, my father tries to protect me. I also guess that protecting me also protects him—that he has secrets he does not want anyone to know. My aunt refrains from shaking her head, and turns to one of the women sitting beside her. She sighs and utters incomprehensible words to a visitor, pointing toward my father with her eyes, not moving her head at all. As though she were whispering secretly... some sort of slander, perhaps. She might be saying to her neighbor that my father is still in love with my mother, that woman whose name is no longer mentioned here and who dragged his name and honor through the mud. And that she... she suddenly goes silent—the moment she sees me standing near the door listening. "Oh, you cursed girl... What do you want? ... Get out of my sight." She scolds me roundly, then tilts her head and falls silent once again, busying herself with the coffee pot, which has started to boil.

Cursed girl—this is my name. This is the name I hear more than "Sarah," my real name. My cursed mother whom my father still loves. Whose picture he keeps under his mattress. A picture folded down the middle, of a woman with an uncovered head. A lock of her long, thick hair covers part of her high forehead. A long, full neck slopes down and is hidden behind the collar of her shirt with its round pearl buttons. In the picture, my mother seems to be formed perfectly. I can tell how she was built and also estimate her height and weight. I can guess at how much I look like her, and how much my body—which is just now starting to mature—resembles her body. She was laughing when this picture was taken. She was young.

3

As he does every year, my father begins with insuring the white mulberry fields in the villages surrounding our own. The square-shaped, three-story *haara*s transform into a huge workshop for two whole months. The eastern side of the middle *haara* is emptied of its beds and furniture, which are relocated to the colder western side. That is where my father sleeps and where my aunt does the washing and cleaning, with help from the Kurdish woman, Maryam. The western side becomes more intimate than before. No guest ever enters this part of the *haara*. Only women, people who live in the house, and Ibrahim ever enter it. During the silk season, my father receives his guests in the inner courtyard under the walnut tree. They stay outside and do not enter the house. That way they cannot go into the rooms to see how the silkworms are growing and maturing. They are afraid. Whenever my father does insist that one of the men come in, that man will begin praying that the season will bring all that the shaykh desires.

They repeat these prayers to ward off the evil eye. It is said that a person is affected by the eye through no will or intention of his own. My father's visitors stand to take their leave and empty out of the *haara*'s courtyard with the first cold breeze the night carries in.

During the silk season, our things are scattered all around. We sleep on the floor: in the dining room and the *liwan* whose doors open onto spacious, high-ceilinged rooms that branch off of its entire length. The last and lowest *haara* is located beneath a courtyard that serves as much of its roof, and beneath which its rooms are lined up like compartments on a long train. The men who come from distant places to work in the wide-open fields sleep in these rooms. My father gives them rooms to sleep in, food, and a little money in advance of their hard labor, to which there is no end.

"They are strong and their bodies are solid," he says as they walk by, and he goes on, "Just like donkeys, they're not good for anything but tilling the fields. Village boys aren't good for anything."

He fears them, for they are quick to anger. They shout aggressively, throw their pickaxes on the ground, take their few possessions and leave right at the height of the season. They know how and when to threaten to leave. My father is then forced to ask them to spend the evening with him in the courtyard between the two *haara*s, which overlooks the faraway coastline and from which the sea looms up, a thin blue ribbon, encircled by a thick green forest of pine-nut trees. Sometimes he offers them a bit of oil to light the lanterns in their rooms. When he is sure that they are all contented and have decided to stay, he stops all of this and goes back to his usual harshness.

Ibrahim, the year-round permanent worker, comes to the *haara* with a box of silkworm eggs and spreads them out in a warm corner of the first room in the upper *haara*. The room is then heated and its walls cleaned and coated with lime water before the eggs are spread out on new layers of straw. Sometimes they spread them out on the inner bark of the mulberry tree trunks and hang them above the heater to hatch them quickly. Maryam helps my aunt light the fire and get ready to raise the silkworms by covering the windows of the rooms with a thick cloth that prevents sunlight from burning them. The eggs hatch, transforming into small worms. Ibrahim, with the help of others, cuts up small pieces of soft, moist, green mulberry leaves and spreads them out for the hungry worms. "Yellah, raise them up high before dark!" my father says in his deep voice while walking between the doors of the upper *haara*, so Ibrahim starts moving the small worms from the layers of straw and tree branches to elevated spots that are prepared on planks of wood and distributed among the *haara*'s many rooms.

≥§

As some of the rooms are being emptied of their furniture for the silk season, my aunt summons Ibrahim to come upstairs and help the others carry the iron stove out. It is a big black stove, which

Maryam cleans out, removing the deposits of soot and ashes remaining inside it from the winter. The men carry it far away and put it down at the end of the inner courtyard. My aunt always covers it with an old rug and hangs brightly colored, shiny tassels from it. In the summer, the stove transforms into one of the many seats scattered near the low wall, which my father leans against while sitting atop the stove's edge, observing the workers' families and shouting at their children if they raise their voices louder than what he considers appropriate.

The workers of the lower *haara* live in a long row of separate, dark, gloomy rooms. The inhabitants of these rooms keep candles lit during the small amount of time they spend awake sprawled out on their mattresses, singing *mawwals* that they brought with them from their villages. They lift their voices in songs of passion and exile, which mingle with children's screams and mothers' curses as the weakening sun begins to disappear behind the faraway thin blue line.

At the end of the corridor separating the doors of the rooms and the *dawwara*, the outhouse stands in the sun. Near it in the midday heat, you can hear the sound of grasshoppers buzzing amid the wild trees that surround its door and small window.

'Ayn Tahoon lives off the silk season. It takes out loans in bills of exchange. This way, the children go to school and their fathers wait for their wages, then pay back their debts after the season's sales. Everyone waits for the season. Work begins as does the countdown, and the opening of accounts that will last the entire year.

"Three hundred okas of cocoons!" my father intones radiantly, continuing, "The season won't be so bad... isn't that so, Ibrahim?"

He claps his big hand on Ibrahim's shoulder. Ibrahim lifts up the scraps of worm excretions and mulberry remains. He gathers them in canvas sacks and puts them aside for animal feed.

"Three hundred okas, this season really should bring enough to feed the whole village," he says proudly, "This time, Ibrahim, you will have a share in the season... A big share... You can set up your own household and marry Shams."

Ibrahim nods his head at the speech given to him every year about what never materializes: a share of the season and marrying my aunt Shams, who is more than thirty years old. He mutters incomprehensibly, while his body remains crouched over the canvas sacks. A share of the season and marrying Shams. Two promises the shaykh makes every year, which mean nothing—except to silence Ibrahim and keep him in the *haara*. The shaykh puts my aunt's life on hold year after year just as he puts my brother's life on hold. It is as though time for the shaykh includes no life but his own.

Visits by merchants and silk brokers increase a few days before the cocoons are harvested. They come and they go but do not start the auctioning.

Everything depends on the quality of the cocoons, how white they are. One of these men holds a cocoon and squeezes its sides between his fingers. If it's soft, this means it's no good. Ibrahim stands with my father. They both talk to the merchant, telling him the cocoons are high quality this year, they are as hard as eggshells, and he shouldn't worry. Meanwhile, my brother spends the silk season in the valley. He pitches a tent in the lower part of the field and we do not see him at home during the whole summer. He divides his time between the tent and his mother's house. This is the best way for him to avoid my father. They rarely meet without arguing.

In the beginning, my father did not raise silkworms. He started this at the end of the First World War, a few months before I was born, when my grandfather—who was my father's age—read about a decision issued by the French, allowing the importation of silkworm eggs to resume. He brought this news to my father, who quickly used my grandfather's money to rent the lands rich with mulberry trees. He also started farming the land to care for these mulberry trees, betting that the cultivation of silkworms would make a comeback, flourishing once again.

The workers relax and turn their attention to the fields during the silkworms' fasts. The worms fast three times and three times break their fasts, all before the beginning of the red, or last, fast, when each worm excretes a silk string that it wraps around itself in a cocoon. Ibrahim comes with the workers and picks up the remaining pieces of mulberry leaves and cleans everything, including the wooden shelves, so that the silkworms do not succumb to illnesses like *deblan*, or *qiyah*, or other diseases whose names I do not even know. These diseases frighten my father, who every morning comes into the rooms where the raised wooden shelves are. He observes the silkworms eating and thriving beneath his very eyes and assures himself of how clean the place is. He observes them in order to be sure that their sizes are adequate and consistent with one another. This is so that after the last fast they can all move at one time up to the tree branches suspended on the wooden shelves and begin spinning their cocoons.

Of all the rooms in the upper *haara*, only Muti'a's remains furnished and rented during the silkworm season. Muti'a keeps to her room and does not travel to Aleppo during the summer so that she can spend the vacation with her husband, Diyab al-Halabi, who works as an Arabic teacher in the English school for boys. Her husband teaches during the vacation as well, giving private Arabic lessons to the English people who live in the village next to 'Ayn Tahoon. He visits them in their houses and drinks tea in ceramic cups and speaks to their women in formal Arabic *fusha*. At the beginning of his tenure in 'Ayn Tahoon, Diyab al-Halabi taught in the girls' school—until the Anglican mission that directs the two schools moved him to the boys' school, at the request and insistence of the young women's families, who preferred to leave their daughters in the charge of female teachers.

The terraces just above the *haara*s are sparse and dry. They cannot be cultivated because it is too difficult for water to reach them. Many ancient mulberry trees grow there. Ibrahim pitches a tent of canvas and cloth there, where he had built a stable for the cattle and my father's horses. When the wind blows, the animal smell enters the windows on the upper side of Muti'a's room, which is no more than one meter above the terrace.

In the beginning, Muti'a was not able to convince my father to build a bathroom adjoining her room in the open courtyard at the back of the upper *haara*. To do this, he would have had to build a door into the room's wall that would lead outside. He didn't want to do this and for years she walked around the upper *haara* to go down to the open courtyard in the lower *haara*. She would wrap herself in a black abaya, cover her head, then cross the open-roofed corridor, passing in front of the workers' rooms, from which they watched her, behind the bars of their windows. Aromas would brush against them, the scent of the mastic, herbs, and aromatics she grinds and mixes to create the perfumes and creams she massages into her milky white skin.

Muti'a calls me into her room and asks me to pour hot water on her shoulders and back. I find her sitting in the large copper washbasin, singing while she bathes. A fractured whiteness like a misty dawn emanates from her body in the pale light of the room. She takes a bunch of her wet hair and begins winding it around itself and braiding it. Then she covers it with a white towel that she wraps around her head, raising it up on top of her head like a *tantoor*.

She stands up while continuing to sing and touches her naked breasts, located high up on her taut frame, then caresses them slowly, like a crystal vase that she is afraid of breaking. She dries them with a small towel and then gets out of the large washbasin where she had been sitting, entering the coldness of the room. The vapors rise from her skin as from the crater of an extinguished volcano. She covers her body in a big cotton sheet and the scented vapors dissipate. In these moments when I see her stand up, getting out of the water naked, I think of asking her about my mother.

"She went to search for her soul," she always answers me, continuing, "We cannot live without our soul... We suffocate... If your mother had remained here, she would have suffocated."

My mother went to search for her soul. I have heard this from Muti'a many times. Perhaps this is why I believed for a long time that our souls could escape from us against our will. They can simply leave and then flee—just as my mother fled—and we might find ourselves on a long journey searching for them.

4

The wooden icebox that they brought that morning is filled with ice. This is the first time that I have ever seen solid ice. I touch it with one hand and find it cold enough to burn my fingers. The cold water that Ibrahim always brings in jars from the 'Ayn Tahoon spring is now no longer enough. The women gathered around the many piles of cocoons drink a lot of water while they work. I see many women: Shakeh the Armenian, Muti'a, my aunt, Umm Doha, and Maryam, along with the wives of the workers. They gather in the morning to cut the cocoons and bring them down from the raised wooden shelves. They then pile them up in large straw baskets and clean off the threads hanging from them.

The cocoons shine in the sun, white and diaphanous. One of the women lifts the terracotta pitcher whose icy water has leaked, moistening its surface and deepening its color. With one hand, she lifts the pitcher over her head, which she leans slightly backward. She opens her mouth a little and tips the pitcher. The water flows through its small opening, spilling out. A few drops of cold water fall on the woman's chin and drip down onto her neck, drawing a line that passes through her cleavage. A short and sudden "ah" escapes from the woman, followed by a little laugh.

Unexpected bursts of laughter recur like a contagion spreading from one woman to another. They laugh and their laughter bubbles up like a spring emerging suddenly from deep inside the earth. The women laugh, then stop, and only a few short words are heard. Their laughter resumes, rising up behind a setting sun that casts a shadow against the piles of white cocoons. They laugh simply, just like that, as though tending to the power of those intimate, hidden places in their wombs that are life itself. Instantly I feel that their faces are familiar, and the sudden tenderness that fills their features brings them closer to each other, making them seem more alike.

The women meet around the piles of cocoons in order to clean them. Doha and I start off working with them, but quickly get bored. We run away, chasing the cicadas and then watching them fly up into the sky. We search for the most beautiful of the colorful cicadas with their phosphorescent green wings. We catch her and make her a comfortable bed out of the dark-colored strings that are wound around harvested cocoons. We put the strings in small metal cans we find in Muti'a's trash. Her husband brings her these cans as a gift from his female English students and she throws them away after she has emptied them of the preserved foods they contain.

Shakeh looks at the empty cans in our hands and says that Muti'a's trash doesn't look like the trash of any other woman in the village.

"How does she have time to cook like all other women?" my aunt says, with a laugh that conceals a certain wariness that she harbors about Muti'ia's lifestyle, adding, "With visits all morning long, passion and moans all evening long."

Muti'a laughs at what my aunt and Shakeh say about her and keeps laughing until her eyes tear up.

My father passes in front of the women, who are sitting in a circle around the pile of cocoons. He does not look at them, as though they are not there. Their voices grow quieter and they hide their naked, outstretched limbs. They sit up straight and fold their legs underneath their long, flowing clothes to conceal them. Only Muti'a does not take notice of him. She lifts her head and looks directly into his face while her hands continue cleaning the cocoons. When he is right near her, inattentively—as though she doesn't mean what she is saying and isn't waiting for an answer—she asks him, "How is the shaykh?"

Then she turns to my aunt and, smiling with cunning malice, says in a low voice, almost a whisper, "Oh, what a waste, a lonely, single man..."

Muti'a smiles when she whispers this to my aunt. My aunt also smiles, a smile of secret understanding that, despite its implicit agreement, bears the remnants of a long-standing censure, which time has not yet quite erased. Muti'a remembers the incident at the root of this: when she met my father in Beirut one day, on her return from a visit to Aleppo. She wanted to hire a car to take her from downtown at the Burj to 'Ayn Tahoon. She saw my father negotiating with a woman near a cheap hotel there. She saw the woman lift her head to indicate no, to refuse what he was proposing. Muti'a left the taxi stand. She approached my father, after using the abaya wrapped around her body to completely cover her head, even her eyes, using it like a burqa over her face. When she drew near him she lifted this covering a little from one eye just enough to wink at him, indicating with a tilt of her head that he should follow her. Then she walked. My father left the woman standing near the hotel and followed Muti'a—not knowing her true identity. She walked a long way from the Burj toward the sea and he kept following her. Whenever she felt him slow his pace, she would stop for a moment, use her eyes to flirt with him again and then keep walking, so that the man could recuperate and overcome his shortness of breath in order to keep following her. She led him round all of Beirut's souqs, took him up to the fish market and the Nuriyya steps, only to bring him back once again to the *waqf* land around the Mar Geries Church. She stopped many times to be sure that he was still following her. She dragged him along behind her like her shadow until she reached the Qazaz Café, which was full of customers, and she stopped there. When he drew near her, she heard him say, "Where else do you want to take me?...

Enough of this." Suddenly, she lifted up her face covering, saying, "You haven't recognized me yet, shaykh?" Then, in front of all the people sitting in the window of the café, she started hitting him with her small leather purse, saying, "You haven't recognized me yet? You still haven't recognized me? You follow women you don't know and then act like you're a shaykh… and a lonely, single man!"

Doha and I get up to many things together in secret. We don't tell anyone because of our great desire to have a secret no one else shares. Perhaps we also feel ashamed of what we are doing. We enter my brother's room silently. Doha opens his wardrobe and drawers. She lifts his shirt to her nose and breathes in slowly. She closes her eyes for a few moments and then opens them a little, saying that she loves his scent. We take out books that are always hidden under his bed. We put one of them inside the big atlas and pretend that we are studying it, when actually we are reading stories of "The Most Famous Wonders" with fear and trepidation. We steal a look at the women and find them distracted, not noticing us at all. We look over at them again and then touch our own soft bodies. Doha slowly and silently lets her hand pass over her breasts… She pauses briefly then reaches toward me, using her hand to roam around my face, breasts, and arms, slowly and tenderly. I slowly close my eyes and relax. We look over at the women in the courtyard again and know that the women in the book look like these women, sitting in front of us, and not like us at all.

For a long time, I think that my brother wrote everything that we were reading and that this is why my father is angry with him. When we tire of reading, we return the book to its place and put colored pins in the silkworm cocoons. We make them into splendid, shining spheres that we use to decorate the hair hanging down over our faces. We play wedding, suddenly remembering that our time for this has not yet come. My aunt starts shouting when she sees us, accusing us of ruining the whole season for her. She directs her words toward Muti'a, with affected vehemence, "I told you to cut off all of Sarah's hair. Look how it's hanging down over her face like the hair of the English headmistress's dog!"

The women finish cleaning the cocoons piled up in front of them. Their hands cease working. The hot *metteh* is passed around. Shakeh the Armenian refuses to drink *metteh*, and asks Maryam for a glass of tea. Hands rest a little in laps. The women stop working, but they keep on talking. The sunset creeps up quickly, followed by a slight darkness, which a cold dampness envelops like a thin headscarf. In this kind of darkness the women do not need to light their lanterns. The kerosene burner, which heats the water in the *metteh* pot, illuminates the little circle. The piles of cocoons in baskets reflect this drowsy yellow glow, and the women's legs stretch out, exhausted and lazy.

Shakeh wants to go back to her country. She constantly repeats this. My aunt says that Shakeh has been dreaming about returning since she first came to Lebanon.

"I fled death, but I look at it when I sleep. I am afraid to sleep..." Shakeh says in her rather thick accent while holding her hot glass of tea.

Shakeh belongs to one of the Armenian families that were relocated to 'Ayn Tahoon after the First World War. No one from her family escaped and survived, except her son, who fled the Turks with her, taking refuge in a mulberry orchard outside the village. In the beginning, the immigrant families that came pouring in lived in makeshift camps on the eastern coast of Beirut. Then they scattered.

"In the camp I saw many of them, families I knew and families I was seeing for the first time. I couldn't approach them and speak to them. I was afraid. I said I want to search for another place and live there." Shakeh recounts this in a deep voice. It emerges hollow, as though coming from far away. "When they started to spread us out, I was happy that I would be going far from them and from the camps that the French had built in the city. I said I want to forget everything and bring up my son Yaacoub. But I couldn't."

"May God punish those responsible," my aunt remarks in a voice rising from deep inside her, while extending her arms and raising her head to the heavens.

"May God send them three things all together: gunpowder, air, and fire," Muti'a calls out in her Aleppine accent and strong voice, as though singing.

"I will return, I will return for sure," Shakeh says and then her usual absentmindedness returns. Her features soften for a few moments and her eyes' intense hardness becomes bitterness and pain. She repeats again, "Some day, I will return and if Yaacoub is stubborn about remaining here, I'll have to slap him on his bottom like I used to do when he was little."

"A child is never too old or too important for his parents," my aunt Shams comments, adding, "He will return with you, he won't leave you."

"Be wise... You believe that you'll be able to return. If you return, you won't find anything. Those who leave do not return. There's nothing to go back for," Muti'a says, immediately adding warmly, "What do you want to go back for? ... Stay here. We would miss you. Who would sew all these beautiful clothes for us? I'm not going back to Aleppo. Whoever drinks the water of 'Ayn Tahoon cannot leave her. Back there, I had a house and a garden. I left everything and came. I thought that it was a visit and that I would return. They took me to see the shaykh in Tripoli. They told me he would cure me of my pains and illness and would lift the curse that was preventing me from conceiving. But this visit changed my whole life. My first husband divorced me and I married Diyab. I returned to Lebanon a second time, I stayed, and I healed. I did not conceive, but I healed."

A light breeze picks up. It carries a damp freshness. The women move from the outer courtyard to the spacious family room inside. Maryam takes the things into the kitchen and starts preparing dinner with my aunt—boiled potatoes, vegetables, and *kishk* in oil. My aunt asks Maryam to bring her the matches, the ones that were on the kitchen table and that Maryam has hidden as usual between the folds of her dress. My aunt scolds her, asking her to return what she has taken. Maryam removes the box of matches from inside her dress, handing it to my aunt and saying, "Really, I only take what I need." Then she goes down to her room from the *haara* repeating, "Piles on top of piles on top of piles... what is all this accumulation for?"

She means that my aunt keeps accumulating things in the wardrobes and in bundles—things that she does not need and does not use, though she guards them, keeping them far from anyone else's reach.

The men have left and won't return until late at night. Only women remain in the *haara*. They sit on the floor in a circle around a big copper tray full of food. My aunt lifts the lighted oil lantern and hangs it on the chandelier with the never-lit candles. My grandfather bought chandeliers and crockery from Turkish merchants. He was proud that his house was furnished like the houses of foreigners and not like those in the village.

Muti'a returns to her story. This is the story of her marriage to a shaykh and muezzin in one of Aleppo's mosques when she was fourteen years old. At first she was bewildered about what she should call him. Should she call him "uncle" because of the age difference between them? Or should she call him "shaykh"? Or by his first name, as all women call their husbands? He entered the house and did not speak to her. Muti'a laughed, saying that he also entered her silently. He used his words sparingly to prevent wasting them... excessive erotic economy... she says. Then she told us how she waited seven years to be blessed with a child. At first, she would wait every month and say that surely this time she would be pregnant. She would look carefully at her eyes in the mirror and stick out her tongue. She took deep breaths. She smelled them. She felt her breasts. Nothing! She looked at her underclothes. She smelled the scent of her period even before it came... and there it was. She visited all the shrines, sanctuaries, and monuments. She distributed offerings, lit candles, burned incense, grew roses, performed her daily *salat,* implored God, beat her chest, and got down on her knees to pray. She vowed to walk barefoot if her wish came true and to pass out cups of *mughli...* but despite all this, nothing happened.

She began to realize deep in her heart that a pregnancy would not happen with this man. And she wondered how it could happen, since she felt that when his semen entered her womb, it curdled and transformed into stagnant water, which could never bring forth any life. How could it happen if she did not listen to a single word he said? Does semen alone make miracles? She knew from the start that something was missing between the two of them; her womb was not moist, soothed, and soft in order to receive him, even though it was as alive as the beating of her heart. But as soon as the man was heavy on top of her and entered her, her womb would close in on itself. She would coil up and shut herself off as though she were on the edge of a dizzying path, high above a deep valley.

Her mother took her to Tripoli. They told her that a shaykh there could cure her and help her get pregnant.

The two of them went to an old house behind a big mosque. They crossed a street lined with many bookshops, then entered a dark alley that daylight did not reach. They went up a damp staircase that had weeds and moss sprouting between its stones. Muti'a felt cold though the weather was warm. She said to her mother, "Let's go back to Aleppo." She said that but her mother had already started knocking on the brass-handled door. A short stout woman, her head wrapped in a thick cloth that looked like a bed cover opened the door for them. Without speaking, the woman pointed to an inner room. They entered a dark room with only a faint light in the middle of the floor. The two women did not hear a sound. They could not see a thing, but Muti'a smelled the scent of a living being. Then she saw him sitting in the middle of the dark room—a man, emaciated, short in stature, his eyes closed. In front of him a kettle of water was boiling on a kerosene burner and a weak light, like candlelight, emerged from it. He removed a book that had been resting on his lap, as he sat with his legs folded under his body. He did not ask her anything, but directed his instructions to her mother, who was standing near the door. He indicated that she should request Muti'a to sit down facing him.

Muti'a approached him and sat on the ground, still facing the door. He reached out and grabbed her shoulders, then started pushing down with his fingers slowly and powerfully. Muti'a felt a pain move from place to place throughout her body. He moved this pain under his fingers, sighing weakly as his fingers traveled, as though the pain leaving her body was being transferred to his own. He then devoted his hands to her sides and started massaging her, moving up and down her arms from her shoulders to her fingernails. His hands proceeded to her back, accompanying his movement with rhythmic words repeated in a low voice, without a pause, as though he were praying. After this, Muti'a heard him request her mother to leave the room. He turned up the flame on the kerosene burner and added some cold water from a brass pitcher nearby. The red flame surged up with a roar, like the sound of a small machine. Muti'a felt the blaze of the rising vapor enter the very threads of her dress and strike her skin. She closed her eyes, allowing the hot, vaporous air to enter her lungs through her mouth. Drops of water slid down the back of her neck. She tried to wipe them away with the palm of her hand, but this made her body only feel damper. Humidity filled her pores and her insides. Hot humidity gushed into her mouth like a flood. Hot humidity cooled off her insides; it made Muti'a feel the desire to cry. A fresh desire, which she had not felt for a long time, forced hot tears from her eyes. She felt like someone standing on the threshold between heaven and hell who wants to enter them both at the same time. The man held her arms so that she could stand; she could barely see the walls and furniture of the almost empty room. She closed her eyes and felt slightly dizzy, but under control. He asked her to take off her dress, which was now moist with vapor and sweat. He handed her a dress that was open in the front and flimsy, like a hospital gown. He did this without looking at her. Indeed, he was busy unfolding a large piece of paper in order to wave it over the vapor. He started moving the hand that held the paper while repeating cryptic words and then left the paper on the kettle atop the kerosene fire.

She dried her body and her hair with a towel that had been folded on a chair in front of her. She put on the flimsy dress while looking at the man's incandescent eyes. He asked her to lower her face into the vapor that was passing through the pores of the paper, which was now damp and cracking. He picked up the paper again, replacing it atop the small pitcher of water, and moving his hand as though he were kneading. He took the dough of what were now small pieces of paper and put them in a little bag, asking her to go home and rub this on her belly, vulva, and thighs. She was then to return to him in one month's time. He also gave her one more small piece of paper, placing it inside a bit of leather whose edges were sewn with thin black cotton string. "This is an amulet for your husband to attach to his undershirt—it shouldn't be far from his body!" He told her this while putting the leather pouch in her palm and opening the book in which Muti'a's mother had left some money.

Muti'a pauses at this point to ask the women seated around her if any of them can guess what was written inside that amulet. She says that she gave it to her husband and then started waiting to get pregnant. But the old man no longer wanted to wait. He wanted a son to grace his life and world, so he divorced her. She wanted to know the secret of the paper folded up inside the piece of leather, so she opened it. There she found words written without dots, copied down on both sides with intentionally sloppy penmanship. Written in crooked handwriting, the words were hard to read. One sentence appeared clearly at the bottom of the page. Muti'a read it easily: "A woman is like the land—if you start digging in her and turn the soil over, she will open up, blossom, and bear fruit!"

5

The year races to complete its never-ending cycle. October colors the leaves diverse yellows blended with the damp hues of the earth. The ground becomes wet with silent, sudden rain, while inside, dryness prevails. Snow does not come to 'Ayn Tahoon and neither does the sea. It is a place between the two. It does not go far. It is a mild place, where even time passes slowly. Time here cannot be squandered; it has no bumps or contours. It is like this place. Disciplined and even. Snow does not come to 'Ayn Tahoon, though I see it every morning through my east-facing window. I see it shining white, reflecting the winter sunlight.

I wake up with a swelling wound around my heavy heart; my body can barely endure it. My body, this substance that is my constant companion, sticks to me and lies there between my days and nights, spreading like decay in warm weather.

My kitten Noosa is sitting near my head. She rests her bottom on my pillow and looks at me. Her breaths brush against me. My aunt comes in and, as she draws near my window to throw open its curtains, starts cursing cats and other animals. Noosa looks at her without interest, as though she is used to her voice. She stretches out her front leg and starts hitting my cheek gently so that I will open my eyes again. I know that it is 6:30 and that the sun, which is still hidden behind the bare wall in front of me, will soon enter through the curtains and hit me itself. The sun and Noosa are the two companions of my melancholy morning, a morning as heavy as my heart and body. My body now rolls like a deflated ball toward the new washstand, which is as white as the milk teeth that I hid in the outside walls, years ago.

I remember when Mrs. Dexter, the director of the English school, saw me holding my small milk tooth in my hand. She taught me that whenever I wanted to hide a new tooth in the wall, I should close my eyes and wish for something special. When I close my eyes like this, I find something other than sleep— a magic spell, which, when it works, causes a happiness I have never felt before to flow over me. I dress quickly, a small knapsack with my books and files in it draped over my shoulder. I leave my room, which my aunt has filled with beds that no one sleeps on, under which she has rolled up a number of rugs inside each other, from which emanate the aroma of lavender mixed with kerosene.

I pass through the gate of the *haara* with my eyes closed. I have all the streets memorized, all the small alleyways, steps, and crossings. I have memorized them and their smells as well. With my eyes closed, I feel that I am so light I can almost fly. I find other places of connection that are better felt than seen. The wind carries the sounds of the poplar trees and the towering sycamore in the big square above the *haara*. I know their sounds, which the changing seasons do not alter. I know that the sounds of the palm tree are different, harsher and more powerful. Outside the *haara*, I am happy, alone with myself. I close my eyes and keep walking. I outpace the pulse that is humming inside me. Walking transforms into a new sensation, always pushing me further. I keep my eyes closed. A light breeze brushes my face. It is the walking breeze, the breeze of the sensation of walking—walking with no goal or destination. Walking has its own sensation. It is here, somewhere inside us. And also deep inside those people who are unable to walk. It is dormant in them, it awakens when they sleep and comes to them in dreams. But what would happen if we lost this sensation? It would be as though we had stopped near a wall and just stayed there. And what if we forgot what we were doing moments ago and where we were going? If we just forgot all that... Suddenly, I trip on polished stones, newly lined up along the edge of the narrow path, and they injure me. I fall, my body collides with the stones. I open my eyes and cry out in pain. I find that I do not have the strength to move my leg.

I must keep my broken leg in a cast for two months. I must not walk at all and must stay in the *haara*, watching life pass in front of me from my window. I am not taken anywhere. My brother comes with a bonesetter, a Protestant from a nearby village. The man enters, his son following behind him. The man tells my brother that his hands tremble and that his son Karim has mastered this job with his father's same skill. The young man prepares a dressing and a soft cast as his father indicates what needs to be done at each stage. When the young man lifts my leg just a little, I cry out in pain. I remember the shadow of his body bent over me, wrapping a bandage and the soft cast around my leg—the shadow left an impression on my face. When he finishes his work, he asks me to stand just a bit. I cannot stand on only one leg. I grab him, holding onto the left side of his neck. He takes me in his arms. Despite my pain, I can feel a pulse throbbing under my fingers. I can also smell his scent, that of someone who has just gotten off of a steamship after a long journey. Something inside me awakens and moves. When Karim removes his arms from my shoulders, I don't move my hand, I want to remain attached to him forever.

Doha, my only friend, comes every day with lessons and homework from school. I devour it ravenously while she furtively enters my brother's room. "Do you miss his smell?" I quietly whisper to her when she leaves the room. She does not answer, but with a shy movement of her hand indicates that I should be silent.

My aunt sits in the winter room near the stove and shells chestnuts to roast on the embers. She shells them with her fingers, which have toughened so much that the heat no longer affects them. The muscles on her face tense up as she takes a whole chestnut between her fingers and blows on it. She only eats the chestnuts that have roasted for too long and crumbled into little pieces, no longer whole. She puts these little scraps in her mouth without displaying any desire to eat them, as though she were simply removing them from her brother's eyes by concealing them in her intestines—the only place which the shaykh can't get to. He gets angry if he sees the shelled, roasted chestnuts shredded in little pieces and scattered on the plate.

"This is not a chestnut—this is the food that the cat spits out! I want a whole, fresh chestnut, not a scrap... a whole one, a whole one... Do you hear me?" my father says, adding, "Dammit, she is fucked by an insatiable hunger, affluence doesn't suit her." Without answering, my aunt withdraws furiously into the room across the hall, next to the kitchen. She sits in the corner, surrounded by locked wooden cupboards containing white satin linens, saved for occasions like weddings and funerals. She wraps her head in a big white *mandeel*, and covers her body in a flowing black gown. She folds her legs under her and opens the book of the *hikmeh* on her lap. She recites the verses she has memorized at the *majlis* in a calm and steady voice, though she doesn't know how to read or write. Sitting there, she seems far away from me as I stand watching, alone and helpless, like a drowning person near a plank of wood.

The voices of my father, Doha's father, and Ibrahim drown out her prayers. He wants to cultivate new fields for planting more mulberry trees. My aunt finishes her prayers, stands up to return to where my father is sitting, and does not look at him as she passes, grumbling, "People are uprooting mulberry trees to grow grapes and olive trees instead. The price of silk has gone to dirt and you're still growing mulberries!"

The skaykh follows her words without listening to what she says; she does not expect him to hear her in any case. She believes that her prayers are enough to atone for all of our sins—my father's, my mother's, my brother's... as well as future offenses that have not even been committed yet. Ibrahim nods his head, agreeing with my aunt's words. He also wants to cultivate olives and grapes and to transform the mulberry fields into fields with different kinds of profitable trees, like olive trees, which he praised to my aunt as being like gold. He wants to fulfill all my aunt's desires, but cannot manage to engage the shaykh in a conversation about it.

My aunt keeps the book of the *hikmeh* far away from us. She hides it in the large wooden cupboard. This is where she keeps the porcelain that we never use, as well as towels, sheets for big parties, the set of linens for the deathbed, and other things needed for funeral preparations should one of our relatives or neighbors die. She also keeps the little bit of money that she has saved in this cupboard.

The cupboard remains locked and the key stays in my aunt's bosom. Once, she forgot to take it out of the cupboard's keyhole. It stayed there. I want to read this book that is preserved there so carefully. Why does she always put it so far from my reach? Why does she say that I'm not permitted to read it, that I'm a *kafera* and that I'm forbidden to touch it? I take the book from its place; I sit where she usually sits. I fold my legs up under me. I open it and am about to start reading... I'm afraid. I feel like the person whose actions reflect all the sins of the world... She surprises me with her angry voice, "May God take you away, you *kafera*... Oh God, forgive me..." my aunt says, seizing the book from my hands.

Every time she goes to the *majlis* on Thursday evening, she hears the women praying say that even a very long time would hardly be an adequate wait for her to become a shaykha like them. Because it would be difficult for someone who has a family like my aunt's to establish the reputation needed to become a shaykha. Her brother's wife is half foreign, a Christian, that is, and disappeared from her home, leaving unanswered questions and a daughter who looks like her. Her brother's son left his studies at the English school and left the silk fields and seasonal work in order to drink and smoke and befriend foreigners. Her brother has never once entered the *majlis* and does not even know what the book of the *hikmeh* looks like, but despite this, the people of the village call him "shaykh."

My aunt reckons that what she needs to become a shaykha is different clothes. So she takes her short *mandeel* off her head and replaces it with a big, thick, opaque, white *mandeel*, which covers not only her head but her shoulders and chest.

"What's the difference between me and the rest of the shaykhas now?" she says to herself, immediately answering, "Nothing!"

She starts wearing long, thick, black dresses. She changes her bearing, lowers her voice, and slows her movements. She starts walking and talking slowly, believing that this behavior better befits her new clothes.

"But everyone around you is a *kafer*, you live with them under the same roof. You touch them and you show them your head and face," the shaykh of the *majlis* repeats to her from behind the screen that separates the women from the men inside the *majlis*.

"What's my sin, if my brother's son likes to drink? He's the one drinking, shaykh, not me. He's the one staying out all night and not coming back until dawn. God help him. May God ruin all those who led him down this path…"

My aunt repeats this over and over, referring to Tony the Australian man who is the watchman and manager of the English school and brings drinks and cigarettes to the young men of the village.

He gives them this for nothing in return. For him it's enough that they stay up late with him and keep him company. They tell jokes and laugh, while he seems lost among them and stays silent. He only regains his friendliness when they play cards. Then his loneliness no longer makes him sad and his silence does not need any words.

My brother takes no notice of my aunt's words. She follows him from the courtyard of the *haara* where he bathes to his room. She lets him know what the shaykh at the *majlis* said. She foolishly repeats her hope and implores my brother to be reasonable and return to his studies. She has to move quickly to catch up to him. He doesn't look at her and keeps rubbing his wet hair with a small towel. From the entrance of the *liwan* where I am sitting, this recurring scene between the two of them unfolds; it is something that I have gotten used to, I have seen it before and I know what will happen a few moments later. Muti'a stands behind me, holding a big pair of scissors, and starts cutting my hair. My bare-chested brother turns to my aunt, who is still behind him, and suddenly pauses in front of the door to his room:

"Auntie, reserve a spot for yourself in the afterlife—I don't want to go there myself, I want to go to hell... Get away from me!" he yells at her after losing his patience and throwing his wet towel on the floor of the *liwan*. He goes into his room, slamming the door behind him.

47

My aunt laments her bad luck to Muti'a, saying, "No matter what I do I can't escape their criticism—I can have neither the world nor the afterlife, I can have neither Ibrahim nor become a shaykha—what more do they want from me?!"

Muti'a laughs a little, while grabbing a strand of my hair and raising the scissors in her right hand.

"Calm down, calm down," she tells my aunt, adding with a laugh, "Don't worry about anything, you're not going to hell. It's no problem for you Druzes, your path to the afterlife is short—you go and come back right away."

6

My brother does not talk much and so I am very happy when he does talk to me. He always says that one day he will leave the *haara*. He will leave it to my father with whom he doesn't get along.

"All of you, tell me! Is this what a man looks like?" my father asks us, in an angry, theatrically raised voice, pointing at my brother as he returns home.

"When I was your age, I used to grind stones in order to survive. And you, what are you doing? You play cards, you sing and drink, and stay out until dawn. The seasons pass and we don't see you. Ibrahim alone stands by my side and doesn't leave me. You have no idea what I go through..."

Whenever my brother comes home my heart shudders. I know that there will be shouting, doors to bedrooms will be bolted violently, then one of them will be opened again and quick angry footsteps will cross the large *liwan*, going outside. Only then do I say that my brother has left the *haara*. And when I hear him slam the big iron gate behind him with all the recklessness that I love about him, I also say that this time he won't come back. My heart plunges and the pain in my broken leg increases. I stay in my place and wait with the anxiety of a prisoner who has not yet been tried. Will he too go out searching for his soul? I ask myself.

Why is it that no one here can stand living in the *haara*? What is it about my father that pushes people away from him? Do I not also dream of one day leaving and not returning? This dream increases the burden of our sins—my mother's sins and my brother's. This burden causes me to grip my heavy heart, clutch my soul to keep it from slipping away. But I dream of leaving and my aunt dreams of convincing my father to find religion, atone for the sins of the people in this house and their ignorance, to become a shaykh and go to the *majlis* and pray.

"*Inshallah... inshallah*," he answers her, with dwindling patience, cutting off a long disquisition she had started on the subject. He stands there in his place silently, lost in thought, and when I come in he doesn't notice my presence. He lifts his head after a spell, and asks me if I know anything about my brother, who has not returned home for the past two nights.

"This time things will change for us," my father asserts authoritatively after a long silence. Without waiting for my answer, he continues, "The boy will come to his senses; he'll grow up and be reasonable, like a man."

My brother is angry when he leaves the *haara*. As he does every time he leaves, he returns to the small family house that his mother lives in, and soon he will return once again to the *haara*.

"You really are my sister, but we're not the

same," he said to me the last time, adding, "Ibrahim has more of a place in the *haara* than I do."

But I really don't understand any of this.

He comes back to the *haara* when my father is away. He hugs me and while he is hugging me I forget the pain in my leg. Karim accompanies him. "He came to check on you," my brother says, pointing to Karim. My heart flutters and I wonder which of the two of them I love more. I tell Karim that my leg hurts. He asks me to stretch it out a little bit. He puts his hand on the upper part of my leg and lifts it. The veins of his hand swell, bulging out right before my eyes. Heat rises from them. His hand rests on my leg long enough for a pleasurable current to run through my body. I am affected by a desire, a blind desire as strong as hunger, to be near him when I smell his scent. He stands up to say goodbye.

"Stay…" I say in an almost inaudible voice.

"I'm going down to Beirut to the university. I'll come back next week."

He asks me to leave my leg outstretched for as long as possible and gives me a book, telling me that reading stories will make me forget my pain.

It is strange, the sight of three men in front of the large iron gate on Sunday morning. They stand behind my brother, who is accompanied by Karim, and wait for Ibrahim to open the gate of the *haara* to let them into the courtyard. Three men in long brown robes like women's dresses. They have thin beards and wear black hats. They enter the *haara*'s courtyard, where the night's rain has gathered on the ground, behind my brother. Karim was asked to introduce them to his friends in the village, so he introduced them to my brother. Karim doesn't enjoy their company, but feels obligated to them because his father worked for a number of years at the missionary center, which made it easy for his son to receive a scholarship to study at the American university.

My brother has not hugged me as he does this time for a long while. It is a warm hug, tender and full of apologies. He brings the men into the winter room, where my father is sitting. Both their appearance and my brother's morning return home are a surprise to him, though no astonishment shows on his face. He invites them to sit down and asks my brother to introduce them.

These are missionaries who came to visit the school. Mrs. Dexter asked Karim to accompany them on a visit to the families in the village.

My father tries to speak to them in their language, English, resorting to the few words that he knows. He tries hard and motions with his hands and eyes. He wants to let them know that he is a friend of the English people, and that he has received many of them as guests in the *haara*. He continues being polite to them, moving his head, believing that this will help them understand what he wants to say more easily. The oldest of the men takes a bunch of books out of the leather bag hanging from his shoulder and distributes them to his companions. He gives one to my brother and father as well as Karim. My father takes his copy while the three men begin turning the pages of their books searching for a specific, agreed-upon page.

"What is this?" my father asks, feigning innocent surprise on his face, while the book remains closed in his hand.

"This is a book of hymns and songs," my brother answers.

"Which songs do you mean?" my father asks him, showing his interest. He follows up by asking one of the missionaries: "Does it have *mawwals* in it? Can I find 'Abu Zulf,' for example? Come on, open up the book for me, sing me this song."

He turns the book's pages while humming the tune of "Abu Zulf" and pretending to search for the song. One of the missionaries stops turning the pages of his book and raises his eyebrows inquiringly.

"No... that's not what they mean, Dad," my brother inserts.

"Where do you find the *mijana* and the '*ataba*? Where do you find the songs we used to sing, where is the young man on the road to the spring? I want a *Rosanna* song... yellah!" the shaykh says and then, as though he hadn't heard what his son said, resumes his humming, motioning toward the open books with his eyes. Karim tries to talk to him this time, but he intentionally disregards him, continuing his song, then pauses suddenly to ask once again where to find this song in the book.

Karim approaches the man and starts translating what my father was saying. The bearded man shakes his head, acting puzzled... How is it that my father has not heard of the hymns in the book? Directing his words at my father, he says in English: "No, sir, no... you won't find any of those songs in the book, though I don't doubt they're beautiful—we respect them. It's a different sort of book, though, because it helps us come closer to God. Its words are addressed to our souls and not our bodies."

My father the shaykh is quiet for a while. He rises from his seat and, like an actor on the stage, starts playing the role of someone whose hope has been dashed: "Who says that 'Abu Zulf' does not bring us closer to God?" he asks in protest without looking at the men sitting there. Then he walks toward the door of the room, wiping his brow and continuing as though he were speaking to himself.

"There are no 'ataba and no mijana. And you call it a book of songs. A book of songs and hymns! What good is it? He said songs... he said it!"

He draws back a little, then suddenly stands near the entrance to the liwan and turns his head in my brother's direction: "And you listen to them like a fool. They've eaten up what's left of your little brain. I sent you to school so that you could get educated and become a teacher. Nothing has come of you. I told you, it's okay, work with me in the fields and during the silk season. But you don't listen. You turn your back and leave. Then you come back to me with a group of missionaries, who I don't know from Adam... He said songs, he said..."

"Oh, what a disgrace for you, Shams, if the shaykh at the *majlis* knew that they came in the house..." my aunt says to herself the moment the missionaries exit through the gate of *haara*. "I can't take it any more, they will threaten to banish me from the *majlis*." With the palm of her hand, she hits her head, which is covered by the white *mandeel*, "I'll deny it and say they were a group who lost their way to the English school and came to the *haara*."

"Your nephew will be initiated and become a shaykh... He is so useless, maybe then he'll find his way, come to his senses and become a respected man." This is how my father surprises my aunt one night when she returns from the *majlis*.

"And him... did he agree to this?" my aunt asks, not believing what her brother the shaykh was saying.

"The important thing is that the shaykh of the *majlis* agrees," the shaykh answers her, dejected. It seems as though the pains he has taken to convince the shaykh of the *majlis* to accept my brother have exhausted him, sapping his strength and leaving him too weak to continue this discussion.

It is difficult for me to imagine my brother dressed as a religious shaykh, in clothes bearing no relation to him—so unlike his actions or way of thinking. Despite this, my brother agrees to try, meaning he will accompany the people who go to the *majlis* on Thursday evenings, seeking the *hikmeh*, religious enlightenment and knowledge. He knows deep down that this won't really change anything, but will only ease my father's anger and my aunt's persistent nagging. I stand in front of the door and watch him walk away with the others, like a lamb being led to the slaughter.

Four times, my brother accompanies them to the *majlis,* and then he disappears again. The last time, he left the *majlis* before everybody else. He took a pair of shoes he felt suited him from those lined up outside the door and left. When my father asks him why he left, he says he didn't like what they were saying and couldn't befriend anyone there.

Karim starts frequenting the *haara* with my brother. He never stays for long. His visits are just waiting, waiting for my brother, who disappears inside as soon as he arrives. My brother showers in the new bathroom next to the kitchen and changes his clothes. Karim sits close to me after giving me new books that he has borrowed from the university library. His even breathing and his smell fill the world around me. I flip through the books quickly and remove slips of paper that he has intentionally hidden for me in their pages. I throw the books aside and look at him. I find that his eyes have been waiting for me and that locks of my hair have been touching his face and resting on his neck and shoulders for a long time.

Is what we have love? The love Doha talks about fills her eyes whenever she sees my brother; she says that her love for him is real. My aunt-who-lived-through-the-1914-war, as she describes herself bitterly, smiles and comments on Doha's words sarcastically, "Real love, real love, what does 'real' mean? Hunger is real, illness is real... but real love, I don't understand you girls."

My father enters and Karim withdraws from the seat next to me that brings us together. He stands up to go sit near the door. Karim's attitude changes when my father is present.

"You don't know anything about him," he said to me once, "him" meaning my father. He told me that the shaykh robbed my mother's father, forcing my grandfather to give him the money he used to buy his lands. Afterward, he compelled my mother to sign the land that she had inherited from my grandfather over to him.

How did my father rob my grandfather? What is the story of this swindle? Why did my grandfather agree to marry off his daughter to a man her father's age? I wonder. But I toss my questions aside and don't believe Karim. In any case, he doesn't know my mother. He repeats what he has heard from his family and the people in the village. I do not want to believe anyone.

7

The air of 'Ayn Tahoon dances like fire; tree leaves, twigs, and dust all swirl around each other. The wind becomes stronger and transforms into a rainstorm, which pushes everything flying around far away toward the dirt road that leads down to the valley. Sounds rush down from the highest fields. The sounds of the wind steal around the *haara* and disperse between the houses scattered along the narrow dirt paths. Jasmine flowers lie intertwined on the ground and begin to dance around the fire. The colors of the walnut tree's leaves fluctuate between yellow, brown, and red and pile up in front of the iron gate as though they want to go out... They wait for one more gust of wind to carry them toward the outside world.

I move away from the window and sit down to rest my leg, which is hurting me. I want to leave the *haara*, to fly like the jasmine branches and the walnut tree's leaves. I miss climbing the walnut tree and going up inside its branches, then jumping onto the small roof built over the iron gate. Jumping up... to the highest place. This is how I can escape my body's cocoon, the pain of my leg, and fly. I closed my eyes, desiring to fly, then I broke my leg—not what I wanted at all. Things happen to us that we don't ask for, like when we ask for rain and it comes weighted down with mud. My aunt appears and welcomes the rain. She says that the earth and its cracked soil have been waiting for this rain. But I see only mud being turned over on the earth, spreading vainly to the narrow roads that slope down to the fields. The lights of the lamps slowly slant toward the edges of the windows, which are barred with strong wrought iron. A weak light emerges from between the bars and casts spots of light on the foot of the outer wall, where it is cut off by successive pale shadows. Lights wet with winter rain and damp air spread out over the ground of the courtyard. One after another, the lamps are extinguished. A thin whiteness fans out over the outer courtyard; it is caused by a full moon that rises in the sky briefly and then disappears when clouds pass in front of it.

The torrential storms uproot the thin trees from the higher terraces and sweep them right down to the lowest part of the valley. They push them right across the side of the mountain. Light breaks above the newly washed trees, piercing through the short distances between the small leaves that bloom in early spring and rock back and forth, swaying as though cradled by the light and wind. There is a silence broken by dawn's colored sounds, those of trees, grass, and drops of water falling gently on the ground—these sounds, rich and varied, far away and close together, lived with the storm that night and remained alone. They remained steadier than the strong, passing winds.

The drops of water fall so gently that we only feel them when we are inside watching them through the window. They touch the face of the earth, which embraces them; from far away it is like a love scene in a silent movie.

Morning light is radiant in 'Ayn Tahoon. I believed for many years that its mornings alone were blessed with such radiance. Yellow, blue, and white—morning colors appear damp and never more vibrant. It is as though the colors of the sun, the heavens, and the earth are as deep as they can possibly be, they cannot gain any more color. I feel that spring has come early this year. I know this not only from the eruption of the springs and the transformation of the earth's surface, saturated with dark red dampness, into its brilliant green, but also from the slowness of the sunset as it casts its light on the *haara*'s courtyard and walls.

Mornings change nothing in my life. Seasons come and go, torn threads reattached by the strength of nature, the strength of living and survival. My life is reconnected year after year; and the vestiges of these connections remain recurring riddles, painful but not fatal. Seasons end and do not return. Nothing returns; I must get used to that. I must get used to the fact that my mother will not return and that my brother, whom I love, is also about to leave. I dread his leaving. I dread being alone with a shaykh, who is a father by chance only, and an aunt whose life is restricted and limited to meetings at the *majlis*. My brother leaving means loneliness. It also means that it will not be easy for Karim to find a reason to visit the *haara*.

8

Things straighten out after the cast is taken off of my leg. A few days later I go back to school. Sunlight floods the center of the big courtyard, while its edges remain cold and shaded, full of moist dark-green plants. The headmistress of the English school puts her cloth chair, trimmed with bright colors, out on the balcony of the school's highest floor, the floor where she lives and sleeps. She stretches her legs out against the wooden balustrade and sunbathes. Her translucent pink skin shines in the sun as do the little golden hairs she lets grow long on her legs. The trunks of the sycamore, mulberry, and almond trees, scattered around the courtyard and right in its center, are surrounded by small stones. Children sit on them during the first days of spring and turn toward the sun, which licks their cold faces, warming them. I raise my face in its direction and hear the headmistress calling to me in classical Arabic, "Come here."

Before this, I had never once visited the upper floor of the school. I had invented images and woven stories in my mind about this place, which is both near and far. Its walls are built out of polished yellow stones, its windows and corners are painted blue, and a red-tiled roof sits atop it. It looks nothing at all like our houses. It is built on a rectangular plan, with numerous doors branching off it, creating the impression that they lead to separate, adjacent rooms. In the nearby village the houses of English people are similarly lined up below its main road. These houses resemble the school building; the foreigners who come to teach us accounting, languages, and history live in them. They involve themselves in all the details of our lives, but we don't get close to them because we don't believe that it's our right to do so. We believe that their lives are different from ours and we won't be able to understand them. We say naively that surely they live wisely and do not need us. They choose to live in our village because it is beautiful and green, reminding them of the homelands that they have left. We say this as we pass by the place that was transformed after many years into a school where they study Arabic, the place the people in the village call "the spy school." They call it this with no hostility or bad intention until this name seems just like any other phrase in the lexicon of everyday life.

The balconies and windows of the English people's houses open out onto a view of the coast, which is often covered by a thin fog. No one ever appears in these windows, as though English women, unlike the women of 'Ayn Tahoon, don't have time to look out of their windows at the world. In the gardens of the few houses that the English inhabit in the nearby village, the trees and flowers are trimmed into squares and triangles, filling up the houses' outer courtyards. With their pruned branches, the trees take on geometric shapes, like austere green statues. I don't know what Doha means when she says that English people's houses look exactly like them, that they also stand erect and earnest, as though created from plaster molds. I find this comment odd and cannot quite imagine it, but I laugh and nod my head in agreement.

"You will come here every afternoon. You missed a lot of school and I will help you make up for these absences," Mrs. Dexter says, leaning down to kiss me. She then adds, "I will teach you math, science, and English. As for Arabic, that's a subject in which you require no help from anyone."

I know that she speaks Arabic *fusha* fluently and that the letters she asks me to deliver to my brother—love letters—are written in our language. I know this without opening a single one, from the outlines of words and individual letters written in liquid blue ink. I can see it through the flimsy stationery she uses. I know for sure that they are love letters from how my brother takes refuge in his room the moment he receives them, locking the door behind him.

In my whole life I have never seen a woman so freckled as Mrs. Dexter—on her face, arms, neck, and legs. There are small brown dots spread all over the surface of her skin, which darkens in the summer, just as her eyes get bluer in the sunlight. How strange she seems when she speaks Arabic with me. I pose a question and she starts to answer with the formal expression "insofar as I can tell." She never answers my questions spontaneously, without this introduction; it seems as though she isn't certain of anything.

The inside of her house is not like our houses at all. It looks like its mistress hasn't finished furnishing it yet, like one of those places that is always in flux, never permanent. It changes from one stage to another, unpredictably and unimaginably. It is an unfinished form of a house, but it feels alive. I relax when I'm sitting near her, with the large wooden table that I write on in front of us. Sometimes this relaxed feeling is missing and a sudden anxiety replaces it. In those moments, I want to leave her house but not to return to the *haara*. Perhaps the dark wooden colors that shroud the rooms of her house cause my anxiety, or perhaps it is seeing her dog, who passes his days stretched out on a small carpet near the heater. His silent look, with his hair hanging in his eyes, distresses me. He seems ill, or at the very least unhappy here, as though he wants to return to England, his native land.

I am not surprised when she mentions my mother's name—everyone knew the woman except me. She tells me that she knew my mother well before she was appointed headmistress of the school. She met her many times at the Porters' house, an English family who were friends of my mother's. She also tells me that this couple helped my mother get the papers permitting her to travel.

"Are you sure about my mother traveling abroad, about her returning to Argentina?" I ask her.

"No… I'm not certain of anything. She promised the English family a last visit to say goodbye before she left. But she didn't show up. The couple never heard anything from her, as far as I know, and never received a letter from her."

Another time, I ask her, "Do they still live here?"

"No… they went back to Britain after their only son drowned in the sea here," she replies.

At that moment, I do not care about this family or their son's tragedy. I want to know the truth of my mother's story. Did she go back to her country, to her first place? Or did she go somewhere else? Is what Karim told me about my father true? What was the weak spot in my mother or grandfather that my father took advantage of? I do not ask the head-mistress about my mother again. The truth remains suspended between Mrs. Dexter's hesitation and my feeling of loss amid the gossip surrounding me.

It does not take long for my father to learn about the headmistress's letters. He says nothing. Then he once again starts constantly repeating that my brother must become a shaykh, come to his senses and renounce the bad company he keeps— including visiting the headmistress at her home in the evening.

"Now I understand," my father says. "He's started going down into the valley every day. He picks green almonds, green fava beans, and loquat and I think he's come to his senses and wants to work with me, but actually he's picking them to give them to the headmistress as a present."

9

The school year comes to an end and Mrs. Dexter entrusts the care of the school gardens and the forest surrounding them to my brother. She wants to travel to England during the summer holiday, to take care of unfinished matters between her and her English husband, who has left her. This would make it possible for her to marry my brother, who doesn't stop going out in the evenings even after she leaves. He doesn't talk about her, but instead talks about his eager anticipation of going abroad—to leave and not return. He will travel to a strange land and start a new life there. It is as though one day Mrs. Dexter was no longer a woman to him, but rather two wings to borrow. He reads her letters out loud to Karim and puts them in the drawer near his bed. He leaves them exposed to the eyes of others, to my aunt's hands and to my father's anger. My father bellows like a madman, walking up and down the spacious *liwan* and rapping his stick against the green tiles with grim vigor. Ibrahim stands at the edge of this room and reads the letters to my father. I can see the two of them from here, up in the walnut tree, where my body is hidden and no one can see me. Everything is visible from up in the walnut tree. Only the *dawwara*, hidden under the high walls of the *haara*, can't be seen from here. I can see it only from the east-facing window of my room.

"Sarah, you are grown up enough now to stop climbing trees. You're not a child anymore, get down from there!" my aunt calls out to me in her shrill voice. Her words embarrass me and I do not answer. But the tree and I grew up together, and I think that what I am doing is totally fine. I jump right up into it and when I reach its highest branch I stop feeling embarrassed. From here I can see everything and no one can see me. I see Ibrahim putting the letters to one side and gesturing with his hands as though he were objecting to something, assuaging my father's fear.

"This is *haram*, shaykh... to break his heart is *haram*," Ibrahim says imploringly to my father, who just stands there, his body huge and taut.

"I know how to take care of the two of them—him and her!" my father threatens, while his shaking voice collides with a recurrence of his wet, sharp cough.

From the window of my room I see the *dawwara* filled with vibrant, bright yellow sunflowers, their proud, long stems standing tall. They stretch out to their full height, turning their faces toward the sun. The sun reaches its zenith and the sunflowers follow it, their petals becoming even more yellow. They never tire of this pursuit and when the sun sets behind the horizon, the flowers bend their necks and wilt.

🐾

Night creeps toward the *haara*, carrying the warm wind of a hot summer. Night enters my room's open windows. In the *dawwara*, Ibrahim, Mut'ia's husband Diyab, and Muhammad Hassan light a fire to roast corn. The fire rises up in the sky and the men stay back from it, reclining on stone benches. Corncobs are stacked up near the wall to become dinner for the families of the *haara* and their children. Ibrahim approaches the fire and crouches in front of it to turn the burning coals over with a long metal rod with a round wooden handle on the end. His face reflects the flame, making him look like an American Indian getting ready to dance.

❧

Time passes slowly on nights when there is a fire. The wives of the workers seek refuge in their rooms, whose doors are left open to the hot night and the voices of the jackals echoing in the valley. Despite this, the children sleep through the entire night without waking.

This is not the first time that I hear Ibrahim, who knew my mother from when she first came to 'Ayn Tahoon, narrate his version of her journey to the workers:

"I swear to God I have never seen a woman who looked like her. Her face was like the full moon. She passed by the edge of the well, her dress sweeping the ground behind her, and a sound echoed like wind rustling through the poplar trees. I was not drunk, no… I swear to God."

Ibrahim insists on his story, denying that he had drunk anything, and sure what he saw was true—that she, my mother, had passed by the well a little after sunset, looked at him suddenly, smiled, then continued her journey:

"Twilight fell. I could no longer tell white from black. I saw a woman passing by with a face like the dawn when its light first shows. She was surprised that I saw her but she smiled at me and walked toward the big sycamore tree. A tall horseman stood there next to his horse. I have never seen such a tall man in my life."

I find Ibrahim's story and the precision of his words somewhat strange. He never changes a word, not even one syllable, each time he tells it. It is as though he is telling a story he memorized years before and has repeated it so many times that he now believes it.

Ibrahim talks and then goes silent. Everyone else goes silent, too. The burning wood cracks and pops and then its small embers scatter on the ground and go out. The sound of the combustion continues for a few moments and after this the silence is finally broken and the conversation that had been cut off resumes.

The school's forest, which Mrs. Dexter entrusted to my brother's care, is a strange sight. Its trees are completely cut in half, down to the middle of their roots. They look like small, naked bodies that haven't yet matured. The old sycamore trees are found cut down the middle, as are the cypress and the pines.

None of the village people know who did this deed and the person is never found. Of course, they have to question my brother, the person now responsible for the forest, and who is taken by surprise, despite reports that claim he had agreed to cut down these trees to make them into charcoal in exchange for a cash bribe, received in advance. But the felled trees remain in their places and no one moves them. It doesn't take long, however, for the news to spread among the members of the English expatriate community and the administration at both the boys' and girls' schools. Their attitude contains an implicit indictment of my brother, despite his denial that he knows anything about it. Mrs. Dexter does not return to Lebanon at the end of the summer and a new director named Mrs. Stevens takes her place. One letter from Mrs. Dexter reaches my brother; it accuses him of betraying her trust. She also tells him that she has been stripped of her responsibilities and position in Lebanon as the director of the girls' school, and that not one of the English people living here defended her. Some of them sent insulting letters raising objections to her behavior and insulting her good reputation. Even the priest to whom she used to send a meal every day recommended replacing her. Mrs. Dexter vanishes from my brother's life for good, as does his hope of moving to another country and starting a new life there.

Despite everything that happens this summer, the missionaries, accompanied by Karim, continue to visit my brother and go with him to see the village families. The priest who lives with Tony the Australian in a small house behind the school's chapel doesn't accompany the missionaries, nor does he visit anyone. He divides his time between the church and the houses of the English people living in the next village. As for my brother, he starts talking more and more about getting away from my father. The summer's events increase his rejection of his father, which has become as out of control as a wild animal, eventually transforming into deep hatred.

"It's my dad, he's the one who arranged everything, him and Ibrahim," my brother says while pacing my room in unabated anger. I approach him and try to touch his shoulder, but his body shudders, pulling away from me and drawing near the window:

"Akh, if you only knew... he likes to hurt people. He thrives on hurting other people. It's his nature."

I don't answer... I wonder what else he wants me to know.

"Your mother didn't want to live here any more after your grandfather died. She told him she wanted to leave. He forbade her. He swore that he would take you away from her. So she stayed quiet. The English family, the priest, and people your grandfather knew got involved. My father seemed to consent. He asked her to sign papers. The poor woman believed that she was signing divorce papers. She didn't know how to read Arabic. She didn't know that she was completely signing away her claim on the *haara* and all the lands around it."

"I don't believe you!" I reply loudly, surprised. I raise my voice as though this will separate me from my brother's harsh and hurtful words about the shaykh.

"Ask my mother. Everybody knows about this, but no one talks about it," he answers, throwing his hatred for my father in my face, a heavy ball that he throws right at me and expects me to try to hold onto. I try to join him as he leaves the room, but I feel too heavy and am unable to move, as though his hatred has paralyzed my body, impeding its movements.

To me my brother is a full-blooded brother, the son of both my mother and father, not just my half-brother on my father's side alone. His face resembles my grandfather's; it is soft like a woman's face. Sometimes I feel like passing my hand across his forehead and chin to feel with my fingers the softness that I have only seen with my eyes. I want to speak my love for him in the language of touch. He is the only man who kisses me. I don't remember my father hugging or kissing me even once.

This is the reason that I say my brother doesn't

resemble my father, but rather my grandfather. My mother's father. I didn't know him either. I was only two months old when he died. He was sitting on the doorstep in front of the courtyard of the house and my mother parked me near him in my carriage with big high wheels. My aunt said that I started crying at the moment he died and that when my mother rushed to see what had happened to me, she saw my grandfather with his head bowed and shoulders slumped. He looked as though he had just drifted off a little, relaxing in the sunshine. His body was still warm. From that day on my mother no longer nursed me. Her milk dried up. My grandfather used to take care of her as though he were her mother. He prepared hot drinks and *mughli* with almonds, walnuts, and cinnamon for breastfeeding.

"He was kind—like a woman," my aunt explains to me.

This man whom they compare with women was part of my father's social circles and mixed with his friends the "*qabadays.*" His magical powers in healing the sick people of the village helped him in this. My mother hardly spoke after my grandfather's death. She became increasingly silent. Muti'a says that my mother did not utter a single word to my father after my grandfather's death.

I fear my father, but I do not fear my brother, despite how rarely he smiles. He doesn't talk much and I don't see him in the mornings except on Sundays. He wakes up late, in a silent mood, and washes outside the *liwan* near the pool in the courtyard. He takes off his cotton undershirt and pours cold water over his head. He washes his face, neck, and arms, then dries his body with a damp towel.

Drops of glistening water slide down his naked back when he bends forward. They slide down, creating a road as long as my loneliness behind them. They slide down slowly and are stopped by his baggy khaki trousers whose waist is held up by a dust-colored leather belt.

I wait for him and Karim to take me swimming in the fields. The water in the *ghabit* there stays frozen even in the heat of summer. I hate swimming but it's my only chance to go out somewhere with the two of them. As soon as my brother gets there, he throws himself into the water... he disappears inside it and just as I start to feel afraid he suddenly comes out and shakes his head repeatedly like a bird rustling the water off its wings. Karim follows him and vanishes into the depths of the water. My heart sinks. I stand at the edge of the water, closing my eyes and forcing myself to think of serious and sad things. This is what helps me throw myself in without hesitating. I throw myself to where I can find Karim, saying to myself that falling into the icy water is not the worst thing that could happen to me, indeed there are much worse things. I manage to come up with a gloomy thought and hold onto it in order to launch my body into the water. I hold onto the thought so I can get in without screaming. It's strange how whenever I want to think of something gloomy, my aunt's face appears in my head. My father also appears—my strong father, my father the shaykh, my father the *qabaday*. Behind these images lies a weak man who conceals in his heart a reservoir of misery and the absence of love. My body plunges through the surface of the cold water and a scream escapes from inside me. Everything inside my head rises and disperses. When I climb out of the water like a wet cat, Karim laughs heartily and looks at me. He hands me his large towel and then, feigning the gravity that I have become familiar with, asks me, "How many fish did you catch?"

10

The shaykh is not convinced that silk cultivation cannot continue to sustain the *haara* and indeed the whole village, and he repeats this every season before the harvest. And as happens every year, Ibrahim loses hope. But he continues working for my father. He is used to the shaykh's uncertain promises. He is used to putting off the realization of his dream to marry my aunt Shams. He isn't given his share from the silk season, because my father claims that after paying his debts, only a little bit of money remains for the *haara* to make it through the rest of the year.

My father is also not convinced that the silk cloth manufactured elsewhere will appeal to merchants and women. He doesn't believe the tales of those who come to the village and say that such cloth fills the city's markets.

He is no longer content with cultivating silkworms in the *haara* and in the rooms around the *dawwara*. So he also begins cultivating them down in the valley, in old ramshackle rooms with roofs made of tree branches and plant stalks. The space devoted to cultivating silk increases despite both the decline in its price and quality and also the decrease in the number of workers, some of whom have left for coastal villages. The new workers leave their families back in their own villages.

So the number of women decreases until none of the wives of the workers, except Maryam, Muhammad Hassan's wife, remains. Despite her exhaustion and physical weakness, my aunt starts taking care of the *haara* herself, with only the help of the remaining women, while my brother and father are absent for the whole silk season, working in the valley.

Like this, the seasons pass, one resembling the other. The only thing that changes are the faces of the working men. Only Ibrahim, who is related to my grandfather, doesn't leave. I am fond of his face. I am fond of how he sits silently with my father for a long time even when the shaykh raises his voice to complain about one thing or another. Every year, Ibrahim teaches the new workers how to care for these small worms, how to clean their living spaces and feed them. But at the end of the season they leave as soon as they've been paid and never return. They start not to like working at more than one task. They don't like renovating the terraces and tending to the planting and irrigation at the same time as working on the silk production. They want to do only one type of job, which to my father is totally unacceptable. To him these tasks are all one complete job and difficult to divide.

My brother comes back to work with my father, who promises to pay him enough for a boat ticket to travel abroad. He begins taking over the supervision of the silk season in the valley, far away from the house.

It is June of third year in which the shaykh relies on cultivating silkworms in the valley; it is the seventh of June when rains suddenly surprise the fields and the seasons.

"Rain in June... This is God's wrath!" my sick aunt repeats, while bringing everything scattered in the courtyard into the house for fear it will get wet. Everything grows dark as though a black veil has been thrown over the earth's surface, separating it from the sky and the sun.

"The end of time is nigh!" Muti'a shouts from her window, while Shakeh hurries to fold the cloth she has custom-made for tailoring in a big straw basket and rushes back to her house near the *haara*.

Loud, frightening sounds ring out nearby, rising and bellowing from the valley below. They then grow more distant and vanish, but before long they're born anew. "That's thunder," Ibrahim says, but my father does not believe him. Relentless, heavy rains.

"This isn't rain, it's a flood," one of the workers counters.

"We'll lose the whole season," the shaykh shouts, summoning the group back to work.

The workers hurry to the valley, gathering the branches of the yellow-flowered *lizaan* bushes that grow in the woods and now are scattered throughout the six terraces, and piling them up in one central place. These are the branches the silkworms live and thrive on before spinning their cocoons.

But the floods, winds, and steadily increasing torrents propel the dry branches toward the bottom of the field. They then fly in all directions taking the silkworms, which are preparing their cocoons, with them as they are thrown about in the terraces below. The water starts carrying the worms toward the dirt and mud, and after this storm they will spin their cocoons in the mounds of soil.

"Where were you? Why didn't you tell the workers to cover the cocoons?" my father shouts angrily in my brother's face. My brother meanwhile has begun to collect the season's branches, furiously repeating my father's words, mimicking his voice, "Plant, water, harvest... hurry up, work, or you're not a man... when I was your age I was better than you."

He throws everything on the ground and shouts, "I'm sick of this, just sick of it, and I've had it!"

My brother leaves the terrace where the workers stand perplexed, with rainwater soaking their clothes. He takes the road that leads upward, pauses, then turns toward my father, who is panting, a stream of water pouring down his head and face. "I don't want to work. I don't want a ticket to go abroad from you. I'll take care of myself."

Then he leaves.

Despite everything that happens that day, the worms finish spinning their cocoons. My father describes these cocoons—their insides a golden coin and their outsides as white as snow.

My brother vanishes once again. He returns to the small family house where his mother lives. He won't forget this rainy summer day. Nor will I.

One day, Karim enters the *haara* and asks me where my brother is. I smile silently; he knows exactly where to find my brother. I have to feed the silkworms. My aunt is sick in bed in the middle *haara* and my father is in the valley; no one remains with me in the upper *haara* except Muti'a, who is busy drying the grasses she has gathered. I let Karim help me. He shakes out the fresh mulberry branches and scatters the green leaves along the planks of wood. The silkworms start eating after a long fast. It is beautiful to have his body close to me, beauty that frightens me. We move into one of the rarely used rooms in the upper *haara*, gather the green leaves and scatter them. We work quickly as though we are keeping ahead of a time that awaits us, a time we are afraid for, that might escape us and be lost. In a moment his arms enfold my body. He faces me. I leave the mulberry leaves scattered and a trembling sigh escapes me. The silkworms, spread all throughout the green mulberry leaves, eat with a ravenous greed. The sound of them eating rumbles like a mix of autumn rain on dry land and the summer rain that surprised us. Damp winds rise from the earth of the courtyard and penetrate my pores.

He brings his face close to mine. He kisses me first on my forehead then lowers his mouth onto my eyebrows and then my mouth. My face comes alive with his kiss. His mouth rests a long time on mine. Love opens its gates. There is nothing to lean against except the outer wall to the *haara*. I have to lean against it, despite its door and windows that open onto the outside. These windows are open to the sky, to all possibilities. But I don't care what might happen to me. We withdraw to the bare wall; I am pressed up against him. I whisper that I can barely lift my own body, my body that is prepared to go to its limits.

A slow, long, hot sigh gushes forth. It rises only to melt amid the sounds of the silkworms devouring the fresh green mulberry leaves. A warm humidity rises in the air of the hall and settles on the windowpanes, darkening them.

Our voices mingle with the sounds of voracious greed. These sounds blend together though Karim's voice rises above them differently this time. My desire for him increases, going beyond the concerns of the little creatures, the walls and the *haara*. His arms remain under my head, near my face. They are soft and fresh like the smell of a child. His murmuring grows louder and discontinuous sobbing emerges from deep inside me. His body relaxes on top of me with one thrust. I cradle him and my innermost desire rushes out anew.

I hear my aunt's voice calling me from the window of the winter room that faces the courtyard. I can barely answer her.

"Sarah... did you feed the silkworms?"

"Yes, auntie..." I answer her, trying to extract my body from Karim's arms.

"Are they eating...?"

"Yes, they're eating..." I say, trying to sit down so that my voice sounds natural.

"Let Muti'a help you."

"Okay. Sleep, auntie... don't worry... sleep."

"Good... very good."

She closes the window, repeating these last words, then her voice disappears completely. At that moment nothing remains except Karim, except us together.

I see his face differently, the face of a man I didn't know before. Only now do I notice the small white hairs on his head.

The moment of love happens violently, bur-dened by words that rush out of him while his body is thrusting. He remains joined with me. A move-ment deep inside me, deep inside my body, which moves with a flexibility and ease that amazes me. A small, concentrated, thick, wet space. His words emerge fiery, choked, and sometimes vulgar, as though I'm watching him fire a machine gun. His words pass in front of my face, rushing by and not entering, like a September breeze rustling the tree branches. Its leaves scatter then the tree is silent again. This is my first experience with love, a love I am not yet prepared to take part in. Was I in a better state then—before this mutual madness that happened between us? I ask myself this question. But I do not know the answer.

I hear the gales of wind from the storm outside; I hear the heavy downpour of rain... The window's glass is striped like veins and my fingers draw a zigzag line on it through which sunlight passes.

"This winter is a liar!" Muti'a says, while looking out the window of her room and then calling out to add, "Don't believe it! Despite everything, it's a liar."

Nature deceives us; it deceives both people and animals. The snails end their fast early. They usually only emerge from their hiding places after the first autumn rains, and the people of the village gather them in canvas sacks to cook them as escargots.

Perhaps nature is a liar. Perhaps it shows everything differently than how it really is. Perhaps nothing can be built upon what happened between us, it's just a pleasant, passing cloud. I do not know. All that I know is that the strangeness of our lives becomes truth and that we accept and live with this. I know that many things happened that year. I grew up, just like that, all of a sudden I grew up. It was as though another soul awakened in me and propelled me outside myself.

I find myself grown up. Karim comes and goes and the rooms and gardens of the *haara* grow cramped for us. Muti'a stands in front of the back door of her room looking at us. Sometimes, I notice her smiling. She looks at us as though she's checking up on us, then just as suddenly closes the door and retreats deep into her room. I do not know why, but one time when she sees me with Karim, she summons me to tell me about my mother. I believed that I had forgotten my mother. I believed that Karim might help me forget the woman whose soul I have been searching for since she left fifteen years ago.

"Her soul was devoted to another person's soul. Your mother was not able to live with her own soul alone. She gave her soul to the one she loved," Muti'a tells me, then adds, while returning her small glass bottles to their places on the wooden shelf above her head, "She was young and didn't know that the soul cannot be given."

Why does she tell me all this when I am standing at the window of her room, saying goodbye to Karim as he leaves the *haara*? I had never noticed before that one of his legs is slightly longer than the other and that he limps. For the first time, I see how his right leg moves separately and is not synchronized with his left as he walks away toward the outside.

"What's wrong with you?" Karim asks me in the long moments of silence that bring us together in his room in Beirut. I am at a loss for words and struggle to remove his body from mine.

"Nothing... maybe because it's hard to breathe, you know what I mean..." I answer.

My sweaty body suddenly grows cold and rigid.

11

My brother's entire life is consumed by the desire to travel abroad. This living, burning desire chases death from him. It is as though his life goes on only because of this desire. He mixes with the English missionaries and the Armenians who live in the village, some of whom have become members of a new political party, founded by one of their relatives. My brother swings between them as though suspended above water and fire, and this tires and crushes his soul. But he becomes neither a missionary nor a member of any party. His fear of my father does not prevent him, though, from asking the missionaries to help him go abroad. They refuse, with the excuse that their help would anger my father, worsening their relations with the people of the village.

He spends time with them, attends their meetings, and then repeatedly brings up his desire to go abroad. He reiterates this desire to travel while my father searches for a young woman—in order to marry him off. In return for her long wait, Doha succeeds in marrying my brother. She is my childhood friend, who left school to help Shakeh with cutting and sewing. She will be a substitute for postponed travel and lost love. She will be my brother's wife.

The dark green marble gleams brightly that morning, the morning of my brother's wedding. It seems to shine even more when Maryam, short and fat, stands on it looking down and letting drops of water fall onto her feet from the damp polishing cloth in her hand. She collected two types of jasmine flowers early this morning and now they open up a little, floating on the surface of the icy water of the blue china bowl my aunt has taken out of the wooden cupboard she always keeps locked. Muti'a threads a sewing needle, letting a long white thread hang down through its eye, on which she strings flowers, making a garland to wind into Doha's hair.

Hamida, my brother's mother, who became a shaykha after her divorce from my father, enters the *haara* through the back door. This is the first time I have ever seen her here. She asks to sit in the small room near the kitchen, where my aunt usually prays and where linens and blankets are stored in the cupboards built into the walls. She sits there near the door, watching the other women dance in front of the bride, who is sitting on an elevated sofa at the other end of the *liwan*. She does not go with the family to fetch the bride. It is embarrassing for her to appear in front of the group and to be in the presence of my father the shaykh. Religion prevents her from appearing in front of the man who divorced her; it is now taboo for him to see or greet her. She asks the girls from the neighborhood to sprinkle the bride with the jasmine flowers whose petals have started turning yellow in the china bowl.

All the women of the neighborhood dance at my brother's wedding. They dance in the *liwan*, where the threads of sunlight pour in beginning in the morning. They dance differently than the young women my age do. They have something else in them, in their faces and the movement of their bodies, which are tired, but alive and powerful. They are full of a force that exceeds pleasure, only seen on the faces of women who have crossed the threshold of forty. Muti'a moves her firm, prominent hips slowly and the sleeves and chest of her blue-green dress shimmer a little. It ripples and falls gently over her body. On this day, my aunt trades her long *mandeel* for a thin one that covers her head and shoulders, letting it hang over her chest down to her waist. She also changes her long, dark clothes for a brown dress that Muti'a gave her.

The English women send things they no longer need to Muti'a, via her husband the Arabic teacher. Muti'a accepts their used clothes, shoes and things as worn out as a life exhausted. She sits down, spreading them out in front of her in a particular order, like a Bedouin woman who prophesies the unknown. She takes each item and describes it to my aunt and Shakeh, as well as the other women who are watching. Her two hands pull out a colored cloth, unfolding it in front of her to see its quality, as though with this motion she wishes to inherit the lives of others, of these English women. She leaves these things in her room, not needed. She keeps them for a time without using them and then before long distributes them among the neighborhood women.

My father, who has begun to feel old and tired, does not hold out long on the day of my brother's wedding. He goes to his room early on and doesn't come back out. He calls for Maryam, telling her he is hungry, and she comes over to him carrying two big cushions to put under his head and prop him up. She leaves a tray of food near him and walks away quickly. My father is angry and calls her to come back and move the food closer to him. In the following days, he receives relatives and well-wishers while lying in bed, as though it had been a huge effort to marry off my brother. When what he wanted was finished, he submitted to the pains of his body and old age.

12

One year passes, another one comes and the life I had thought was interrupted—its present unconnected to its past—weaves its threads together independently of me. It endures in the vast expanse of time and I pay no attention. Perhaps I do not care and perhaps my life has just accumulated like that, as though this life takes place in and is even born of a faraway time, more distant than the present. There is no use continually trying to sketch out my mother's life and history. She has a history, surely there is a history, but I do not know it. I will not be able to fill in the contours of a life that I did not witness and did not live. It is an absent history and I must simply get used to its absence. But I'm not used to it yet. Perhaps it's because of this that I am now recording my story.

The priest; the English couple; Mrs. Dexter, who left without telling me anything; the shaykh, who knows and does not tell; my aunt, who is trying to reserve a place for herself in the afterlife; Ibrahim, whose silence costs him his dream of being with Shams; Shakeh, who is waiting to return to Armenia; Muti'a, who talks as though she were writing a novel; my brother, who dreams of traveling abroad and never leaves; and Karim, to whom I fled in Beirut out of loneliness after I moved there to study. I fled to Karim without giving him my soul.

These people and their fragmentary stories about my mother... I do not know where to begin. Should I begin where Mrs. Dexter left off? Begin by searching for the English family? Or with Ibrahim's story about her? Perhaps the story my father hints at to convince everyone that my mother ran off with another man. If that were the true story, how could a man called the "village *qabaday*" accept that his wife had abandoned him for another man, without any reaction? Would he simply let her go off, just like that, without inflicting any punishment?

I do not know where to begin. I go into Muti'a's room and see her filling her shelves with small glass jars in which she puts homemade salves and creams. She promotes her craft by selling them to the women of the village and its visitors as well. "This is to lengthen your life and preserve your youth," she says proudly, pointing at a small bottle on a low table near her bed.

I leave Muti'a organizing the small magic bottles that prolong youth and go to see the shaykh, who lies on his bed and no longer leaves his room. He entrusts the care of the fields and the *haara* to my brother—whose anger wanes in the period just after his marriage. My brother assumes a responsibility he never asked for. Matters concerning the fields and the silk, like other things in his life—his marriage and the fact that he remained in the *haara*—make him feel as though he didn't design his life himself, that others designed it for him. My brother cannot find a way to escape—even from his hatred of my father, which increases every day.

The production of silk, the burden of which Ibrahim starts to take on all by himself, decreases in intensity and is confined to the valley. When the land isn't loved, this makes it sick and makes the trees and valley sick, my father says, distressed by my brother's neglect of the silk production. He adds that the mulberry trees that he planted previously are no doubt now turning into wild mulberries and that a tree untouched by human hands becomes savage. When he is weak just as when he is strong, the old man never stops nurturing in his son a deep hatred for him. This dwells in my brother's heart forever.

The shaykh's rule grows weaker and the acreage of his lands becomes oppressive to him. He forgets or pretends to forget about his extensive far-off lands, for no reason other than his inability to get to them. The nearby *dawwara*, encircled by the lower *haara* on three sides, becomes the extent of his fields. He now shouts from behind the iron bars of his window at the workers' children when they come near the loquat tree, whose branches almost pass through the window of his room and live with him. He can no longer stand on the roof of the *haara* and indicate the vastness of his lands by shooting bullets from his pistol to each of the four sides of his property. This is how he once illustrated the borders of his land, while smiling and looking into the eyes of his frightened visitors. Now, he stands in the doorway that leads from his room to a small open patio. He extends his right arm, holding his walking stick in his trembling hand, and points at the boundaries of his property, which can no longer be seen from the *haara* because of the proliferation of houses. In his case, it is not only the new houses that obscure his view of the fields, but also his weak eyesight. His visitors nod their heads, pretending to pay attention and agree. They do not hear what my father is saying, but perhaps are thinking that his horse tied up at the other end of the *dawwara* has also become senile and decrepit, and that his face has started to resemble the face of his owner.

The few times that my father crosses the *liwan* between his room and the kitchen or the bathroom, he carries his walking stick with him and will not risk leaving it behind. His steps have become slow and have lost their strong, lively rhythm. The piece of rubber attached to the end of the stick melted during his last walk out to his land, and its wood now screeches against the tiles like the slow snapping of a huge tree root.

My father grows old; my brother has children. I leave to study in Beirut and during my intermittent vacations I return to 'Ayn Tahoon, finding that the shaykh's control over things has weakened considerably. As my father grows old, the mulberry trees grow old with him and the silk seasons start being hit by illnesses we have never heard of before. In the last silk season, the brokers left the courtyard just as quickly as they came, departing for good. The harvested cocoons are left hanging in the baskets for several days, during which my brother implores Ibrahim to find a way to sell them. But the brokers won't agree to buy them, claiming that the cocoons are soft and yellow. My aunt leaves her room and starts circling around the baskets carefully lined up in rows near the outer wall of the courtyard. She makes sure that they remain out of the heat in the shade of the walnut tree. The baskets stay there and no one buys the cocoons. Butterflies start to emerge from them, flying from the courtyard to the skies like dancing stars. At first small groups of them leave, then they increase until they cover the sky. Afraid, my aunt rushes out screaming to Ibrahim to come. She still remembers when during the War of 1914 the skies of the village were covered by locusts that ate the fields and denuded the entire earth. That very same fear returns to her as she hurries outside, but her alarm subsides when she is sure that she is not seeing locusts, but silkworm butterflies. She starts circling the baskets. These circles make her look like the little butterflies ascending to the skies. Short quick circles, like the movement of lighting a matchstick. Suddenly, her heavy body collapses onto the ground, bursting into tears. Her loud sobbing rises, flushing out the butterflies, and when she sees Ibrahim approaching her, she lifts her tear-soaked *mandeel* from her head, exposing her long white hair. She winds her *mandeel* around her hand into a hollow ball and throws it far away. It flies only to land right in the middle of one of the baskets. In a voice choked with sobs, she then says, "What do you say, Ibrahim... Do you still want to marry me?"

In the baskets, left under the midday sun for many weeks, the soft, split-open, empty cocoons accumulate, then just as suddenly shrink and dry up.

I enter the shaykh's room and look at him. I find that his eyes have become lighter in color, as though they have faded. I swallow the lump in my throat and feel that I have become older than I can bear. I look at him again, as though looking at a distant scene in a book. I take a picture of my mother out from under his bed, the only picture of her that he kept after she left. I take it without pity. I hide it on me without him knowing and I leave.

I am searching for a missing woman of whom I have no memory except a picture that I took from underneath my father's mattress without his knowledge. It is thin and yellowed, its grayish color faded. When he loses it, he shouts at Maryam, accusing her of stealing.

"Honestly, I didn't see a picture..." Maryam tells my aunt, who waves her hand around in the air to indicate that Maryam should pay no attention to what the old man says. Ever since the failed silk season when the butterflies emerged from their

cocoons, my aunt no longer cares about him. He
continues calling for Maryam and cursing her.
When she is fed up and cannot take it any more,
she comes to him with a folded picture and puts it
in his hand.

"Look, I found you the picture."

My father takes it. He opens it and looks at it for
a long time with eyes that can no longer make out
shapes and colors, telling me that he had been sure
that Maryam had stolen the picture from the
moment it had gone missing. He tells me that he
thinks about my mother all the time, and that sometimes when he feels as though she has just gotten out
of bed, he touches it to find it still warm. I look at
the paper in his hand. It is a black-and-white picture
of the singer Asmahan, which Maryam cut out of a
recent newspaper and gave to my father.

He points at the picture, saying that it is my
mother. Maryam signals to me with a conspiratorial
smile, and when she finds that I don't care about
her secret, she exits the room quickly, leaving me
alone with my father. He suddenly asks me if I see
her in my dreams as he sees her every night, adding
in a quavering voice that I should not wear myself
out searching for her because I will not find her. I
look at him and wonder if there is still enough time
to talk to him about my mother. But now I find that
I have already inherited everything he still has of
her. He still remembers so much about her, but he
is losing his memory every day. The memory he

keeps all to himself burdens him and when he wants me to share it I no longer want to. I no longer want to know from him what he did to my mother. I refuse to let him explain it to me. Perhaps this is what torment is—not to find anyone to share our memories with. This man won't ever be able to hold onto one whole, complete story about her. Indeed he couldn't hold onto my mother. She fled before he could own her. And now here I am preserving her picture. She now belongs to me alone. It is as though I am freeing my mother a second time.

13

Karim will travel abroad with a British company, searching for oil in the Gulf. First he has to study in London for two years, training for this work at an institute, and then he will move to the Gulf. He never thought of going abroad, but now he will go. In the meantime, my brother will search for work in the city so that he can leave 'Ayn Tahoon.

"What's wrong with you?" Karim asks me again in his room, the place that brings us together.

"Take me with you... I can search for the English family there, the Porters," I answer him.

Karim is silent for a few moments, then says, "The important thing is for you to speak to your father. Your mother, forget her—that's finished. Ask for your right to inherit the fields and the *haaras*."

Karim says all of this timidly, afraid to appear as though he is asking for something for himself. He tells me that we will travel together, but that my marriage to a Protestant might put an end to any hope of demanding my right to my inheritance, and that before anything else I should speak to my father. Traveling with Karim to search for the English family means marrying Karim. I will marry him but I will not speak with my father about either my mother or my right to the inheritance. I do not own anything; I am not able to own anything at this moment.

The wedding party is simple. Only a few people attend, Karim's mother and his friends, and from my family no one except my brother and his wife Doha. Muti'a and Shakeh come, too. My father the shaykh, who has really aged, does not come. My aunt refuses to attend. I was not expecting them to come in any case. I have not seen Doha in a long time and when I see her I feel that I no longer know her. Her face has changed. She has become clumsy, ordinary; her body has rounded and she has started resembling all other women.

I leave Beirut for England with Karim. I say that this is how I will forget everything... I will forget everything. When I hug Muti'a, I whisper to her, "I will commit my soul to no one."

Places change but we remain in our first place. We have no control over what moves us. It is as though everything that happens to us also remains in its place. Perhaps it is better to leave ourselves and go. To be like a light, mild perfume, like a cloud abandoning the water that pours out of it.

I thought that I would start a new life abroad, a different life unlike this lonely one. But I feel that moving has only increased my burdens anew. I have started to feel that my life now is no different than it was, except that it has left behind me a longer trail of loneliness and an unreachable accumulation of time.

I say that perhaps it is thus that our lives are formed, while we are distracted and we have no say in it.

I search for the Porter family in England. I pay no attention to the small, furnished apartment that Karim finds or to the color of the sheets he has bought. The first thing I do is board a train going to Southampton, where the English family lives. I do not know much about this couple. I know both their names, that they were both in Lebanon, and that their son Malcolm Porter drowned in the sea. I know that they were close friends of my mother and that my mother was teaching Mrs. Porter Spanish. That is all I know, but perhaps there is more to it. The train passes through the forests surrounding Southampton, the leaves of whose giant trees fall and scatter, transforming on the ground into an undulating cover of yellow, crimson, and wine red. Despite this it is still summer; autumn starts early here. It starts in the middle of summer—when my aunt in 'Ayn Tahoon has not yet prepared the winter food stores. The train passes through towering, brightly colored trees. They seem like finely sculpted statues, rising haughtily into the sky. I see old men and women sitting on faraway benches in the forest's park. They sit silently, as though waiting for their time, which has not yet come.

I finally find the address of the English family, a small house located behind a building where many of the town's university students reside. I find only Mrs. Porter and a young Asian maid. The young woman tells me that the Mister died years ago and that the Missus has trouble concentrating, her memory weakened after her son's drowning. She surprises me by asking if I am a relative of the lady, pointing out our considerable resemblance. I pay no attention to her question at the time; nothing means anything to me except knowing my mother's fate. When Mrs. Porter starts talking, she seems incoherent and scattered, as though unaware of what she is saying. She grows quiet for a little while, then starts speaking again. She repeats what she has said, even though I am asking her different questions. She doesn't know who I am and isn't able to remember anything at all about 'Ayn Tahoon or about my mother. Then suddenly she talks to me about her son, believing that I am my mother, "You should have become his wife except that the sea came and stole him from you." She says this, then is silent. I follow up with more questions, but she does not answer. I get up to say goodbye and in front of the door to her house she breaks her silence, asking me to return to my country and visit the priest who was my mother's confidante. "Perhaps she entrusted him with something pertaining to you," she says, then after a second's pause, finishes talking about things that have no relation at all to what she said previously. She goes back into the depths of her house to bring me money in exchange for the milk she receives every morning, believing that I am the one selling it.

She remembers the name of the English priest

in 'Ayn Tahoon, that old priest, who is more than eighty years old. How could I not have thought of him all of this time, despite what my aunt constantly repeated about his visits to my mother and how she went to his church behind my father's back to pray and take communion? What did my mother leave with the priest? Why did Mrs. Porter say that my mother should have become her son's wife if he had not drowned? Did he drown before my mother's marriage, compelling my grandfather to marry her off to my father? Is this the missing link in my father's continual stealing from my grandfather and thus also from my mother? Am I Malcolm Porter's daughter? Is this why I look like the old lady? New questions about my mother's story exhaust me—my sense of loss grows more intense and my uncertainty greater.

I return to London from Southampton, compelled by the desire to return to 'Ayn Tahoon. I came to this place believing it far enough away for me to feel calm and now it is pushing me to a place that is closer.

I want to return to 'Ayn Tahoon, but I remain with Karim. He must be in residence at the institute for a certain number of days. I stay in the small, furnished apartment in which I own nothing but my own clothes. I eat off a plate that is not mine and I sleep in a bed that I did not choose. I cannot acclimate to the thick fog that envelops the city. The cold pierces through my clothes the rare times that I leave the apartment to buy the few things I need, then return. I'm not used to the dark walls of the apartment in which I live. I don't know if this is how they looked originally, or if the soil of time has overtaken their true color. I find that leaving the bed neglected and unmade, the plates and cups unwashed in the sink, is more in tune with the gloom and melancholy of the place.

Karim returns from the institute only to leave again. I wait for him to come back in order to hear a human voice, someone speaking to me in my own language. My head remains on his chest and he embraces me while continuing to talk. I hear him say that life in the desert will be hard, but he will go there and only return once he is rich. I say that I want to return to 'Ayn Tahoon to see the priest; he asks me please to stay longer and repeats that I first should have spoken to my father about my rights to the inheritance—my right to the *haaras* and the fields. He says that seeing the priest will not change the reality of my life one bit. He tells me that next time he returns he wants to see a child of ours growing inside me.

14

Karim travels to the Gulf and I return to my first place with a search that has not yet ended and a new story that I will add to the stories about my mother.

I have seen neither the shaykh nor my aunt since my marriage and I do not know what impact my return will have on them. The letters I receive from my brother while in London do not encourage me to go see them. My brother writes that my aunt does not want my name mentioned in the *haara*, especially because I married a Protestant, thwarting any hope that Aunt Shams could become a shaykha of importance among the female believers. In the village near 'Ayn Tahoon, I try to get used to living with Karim's mother. I do not know how to spend a full day with her. I can't get used to it. I approach her saying to myself that this old woman was once a young woman; she carried Karim inside her body and lived through his childhood. When I get a little closer to her I see that she is lonely like me; loneliness is always my companion, so why shouldn't the two of us be together? She opens the Bible and prays. She prays for Karim. I hear her voice and I do not listen; indeed I think about him only in the moment that I approach her room. Between silences, between worrying and waiting, the old woman reads softly—her voice is feeble and dispirited, it breaks easily. The old woman prays. Her tranquil prayers erroneously suppose that things are stable, that I can rely on a strong, incontrovertible feeling of security, that my death is as far away as she is old, and that I can live with loneliness, the illness that does not kill.

The woman feels my loneliness and reaches out to me with a small book in her hand, saying, "Take this and look at it, my daughter, look at how hard life was for the Virgin Mary, blessed be her name."

I let out a long sigh and answer her without taking the book, "Look at me and how hard my life is."

I go out into the small courtyard in front of the house. The woman insists on calling this place a garden, though it is all dried up, the roses and flowers in the flowerbeds completely desiccated. A dry garden, and an old woman who does nothing but wait. I think about the priest, whom I have not yet visited. I consider visiting him and then I change my mind. It's as though I am afraid of what awaits me there, as though what I will hear will confirm the finality of my loss. It is one step closer to the story and I find myself returning to where it began. I change my clothes and go out, carrying my small suitcase. But I return again to the courtyard in front of the door of the house. I say that perhaps there is news waiting for me. I will find a new truth in the priest's room. But just as quickly, I change my mind. A new truth? What will I do with it, I whisper to myself, and go back into my room once again.

When he is absent, Karim sends me letters. In his work for the British company, he turns over the insides of the desert searching for oil. "Sand transforms into gold in your hands...!" he writes to me. "It's like in fairy tales... like the stories of the jinn," he continues proudly, as though the gold had already become real between his fingers.

Sometimes I find it hard to read the letters—sentences without commas, without periods, as though he were writing without inhaling, without taking even one small breath.

Karim comes back only to leave again. Between his return and his next trip, I spend my time emptying suitcases and filling them back up. He wraps his arms around my body, holding me to him and saying, "This trip I will succeed." He has been saying that for years now. A second and third trip followed the last. Karim wants to succeed, to amass a fortune and then return. He wants to return and find a house full of his children. But I do not have the courage. I dream of a belly that grows round and rises, but I do not have the courage. Karim wants to return and I want peace. But I have no peace. His traveling makes me anxious. This constant movement makes me anxious, not because I fear that he won't return, but perhaps because I've gotten used to a life of little movement, of little life.

The scope of my waiting expands. I remain in bed and do not go out... After days like this, I get up and promise myself that not one more day will pass with me still in bed. I wake up with the sun and walk, not waiting for time to pass, like a train whose seats are all full. I wait for his letters. I reread them. I discover that I am more drawn to his handwriting than I am to him. His handwriting opens the door to travel. I travel while reading his words. I feel the places—I see and smell them all while in my room, on my bed.

His letters become longer. I read them while lying on my bed, which hasn't been made for many days. Behind the bed is a dirty, bare wall. I do not see how dirty it is until that morning. I stop noticing after a long period of time, the same one during which Karim's letters get longer, change, and transform from love letters into a traveler's diary. Writing that is appropriate and perfectly ordinary. I search in the pages of his letters for a line, a word, a syllable that discloses something personal and intimate. Sometimes I search blindly to confirm his absence or definitively prove that Karim can't give me what I'm searching for.

His letters make me happy. They have become like a lung that helps me breathe, they are the threshold through which I travel. But whenever the scope of my wait expands again, I withdraw. When he returns, a silence between us also returns.

"Write to me," I told him last time, as he unpacked his suitcase and put his things away in the wardrobe. I repeated my request bitterly. "Write to me now…" Then I cried.

I ask him to write like someone searching for salvation or for a *roqiya* to protect me from pain. I ask him to write, searching for a love that is self-nourishing—a love that takes one step closer to the dead end that awaits it, even as it waits for a cool downpour in order to be reborn.

I observe him and think about what his love gives me. I feel my body; I love it and see that it is beautiful. I pull away from Karim a little; I pull away but remain where I am… near him. I say that he is far away despite the closeness of our bodies; I say that we live desperation and death in the same way that we live love, in extreme loneliness. My desire vanishes, our bodies move like cold, silent things crashing on the ground with a heavy thud. I tell him that there's not enough time for us to be together and that perhaps we need a longer life in order truly to realize our desires. I wait for him to answer me. I turn toward him, finding his eyes already closed and the rise and fall of his breath already regular. I hug him with the bitter taste of loss in my mouth, as though our life in the end were a mathematical problem, which we may or may not be able to solve correctly.

I ask for words; I believe words are needed to fill the silence, through them I search for a bridge to reach this man. Nothing. I ask for words to weave the imaginary ties that bind me to him. The silence, which takes on different meanings—at times filling us, at other times emptying us—has now taken on only one meaning. I go out into the courtyard of the house and water the jasmine that I planted recently, finding its leaves invaded by yellow. I tell myself that this yellow must have just happened suddenly and that when its roots better grasp the soil, it will revive and turn green once again.

A new letter from Karim. His letters and words once enchanted me. I believed that I could build my home out of them. But it now seems that letters help us to forget their authors, bringing our passion to its end, freeing moments of passion from their eternal prison to flow out onto the pages, and then dry up.

I wait for him and he does not return, I wait all these years like a person who digs the foundations for his house in empty space. I miss him when he leaves; I miss hearing his voice as he reads me his letters and I want to quench this longing through the gates of love, through my eyes and ears. But when he returned the last time, I had gotten bored. I tell him that we should put an end to all of this, all the pain, that each of us should travel down our own path. I say these things at times when I am clinging to him with a blind ferocity, one that pushes me one step further toward separation.

I see now what brought Karim and me together: we were the same—two people swimming along the coastline and never going out deeper. But I no longer wish to merely swim along the coast. I've started wanting something else. Perhaps I discovered my need for some things late. I discovered that the letters I read were not necessarily written for me. Perhaps Karim wrote them to himself and then decided to send them. Or perhaps he wrote them to a friend in a faraway country and changed his mind at the last minute and sent them to our address.

15

I am pregnant and I must wait seven months for my daughter to be born. Only children tie us to places. This is what I was thinking when I left the doctor's clinic. But places did not tie down my mother. She went searching for some other place. The place did not tie her down and she did not shield herself from a desire residing in her soul. My daughter's birth means returning to 'Ayn Tahoon, to the very place that failed to hold onto my mother.

I go back inside and gather some of my things. I take his letters, my only connection to the world. I reread them and put them in the bottom of my suitcase. I think that perhaps I need to read them again; I'm not sure. I gather my clothes and return to 'Ayn Tahoon, leaving a mailbox behind me filled with Karim's letters and accounts of his daily life.

I return to the *haara* as though I had never left it. I return to my first pahulace. I ask myself if it is right to refer to it as my place. I lived here, alienated from the place. I lived a longing for a place I did not know and I remember only as a gentle, fleeting vision, or a memory many people had used before me. Perhaps this is how memory comes to us, after it has traveled the roads that many people walked on before us.

I return to the *haara* and find that I am too late.

The small room attached to the school church in 'Ayn Tahoon has burned down. The old priest left a lit candle near the door and fell asleep. His room burned down. Tony the Australian got him out of the room's low window. His face was blue and his mouth was open. The priest died choking.

The priest dies before I can see him and before I hear my mother's story.

It was almost as though I were waiting for the priest to pass away before returning.

A torment inside me stops me and pains me. Why do I suffer when I love and why do I suffer when this love escapes from me, as though I'm having labor pains, as though I'm giving birth for the thousandth time? I love and fear endings, so I anticipate them. Fear consumes my soul and keeps me from enjoying the journey; fear prevents me from moving toward endings. I turn my back on adventure just before landing right in the middle of it. Why didn't I search for Mrs. Dexter when I was in England? Why didn't I accompany Karim to the Gulf? Why didn't I give him the child that he wanted from the beginning? Why didn't I visit the priest before the accident that killed him?

I have returned to the place that I have not been cured of. I have believed for many long years that my distance from the *haara* would help me to heal. I now understand that we carry our wounds with us wherever we go and that changing places does not heal us; indeed this is our eternal malady.

It is only now that I know how to talk about loss. Now I know that the power I had to choose my life's path was sheer weakness. I chose swimming close to the shore because of the power of fear, the fear of going deep, the depth of fear itself. The fear of love and of my attachment to following my mother's stories to their ends, the fear of being far away and returning, the fear of being tied to a place. A fear of loss. It is as though I suffer, fearing greater suffering. Despite all this, I still have a powerful desire to travel unknown roads—roads to unknown places, roads that lead nowhere, roads that are like the love that at certain moments in our lives rushes toward us inexplicably. A love that takes us and then gives us back. We may return changed. We say that we want love, even when we know it is a love destined to end. It does end, but despite this we carry on.

I return to the *haara* and I see that everything has changed. My brother's wife has not set foot in the fields and never wants to visit them. As for my brother himself, he is still waiting for the chance to travel abroad. He asks if Karim could help him get to the desert as well, to search for black gold.

"But the gold is here!" my father says, lying on his bed and raising his voice weakly.

"Your son has stopped knowing the scent of the soil," my aunt remarks from her seat on the tiles of the *liwan*, picking through the lentils. She does not speak to me at all, as though I were not there. She looks up at Doha standing near the door of my father's room. Then she looks again at the tray of lentils in front of her and says, her hand not pausing at all, "Who would marry a woman who would ruin his whole family? This is what your son did."

My father closes his eyes then opens them again. It seems as though he has finally let weakness conquer him. He is too weak to move any part of his body. Only his eyelashes flutter—slowly and with difficulty. While lying on his bed without moving, clearly debilitated, he repeats what my aunt said about Doha and adds derisively, "She's too good for the scent of the soil...!"

My father speaks and then is silent, as though pronouncing what would be his last words. He opens his eyes and then just as suddenly closes them again. The few times he gets out of bed are only in the morning hours. Maryam helps him; she starts spending most of her time in the *haara* helping my aunt, who has stopped caring that she steals things from the house. She entrusts her with taking care of the old shaykh, who now calls out for Maryam day and night.

Doha was the first person to bring plastic containers to the house. When my father grew old and started losing his mind, he poured milk into one of the containers and put it on the fire. The plastic melted and the milk poured out all over the kitchen floor, mixing with the melted plastic. Strange smells rose up while Maryam rushed to help the shaykh, putting him back in his room.

I go into my father's room and sit on the empty chair facing him. I find him just as he was—he has not moved since yesterday—stretched out on his back. He opens his eyes and speaks. He speaks without looking at me and I do not know if he is talking to himself or if he senses my presence. He closes his eyes again, saying that Maryam doesn't take good enough care of him and that yesterday she left him in the bathroom naked after pouring cold water on him. He complains that my aunt ignores his calls on purpose just to make him angry. He talks about Maryam again and then pauses.

He repeats what he said and prays for her to fall ill, "May she get old and be paralyzed like me, that cursed woman. She wakes up and springs out of bed like a rabbit and I can't even move my body from one side to another. I struggle and try to put my hand under one side to turn over but I can't. I shout out to her from under my covers, 'Maryam... Maryam...' but she doesn't come to me. I see a far-away shadow. I know that it's her getting dressed. She unfolds her skirt and tries to subdue me. She lifts her skirt with both hands, holding it right front of her face, inspecting and contemplating it. All of this is only to subdue me. My mouth dries up, I have no energy left, and only then does this cruel woman ask me, taking her own sweet time, 'What do you want?' She asks me this coldly, just like that, when I'm about to die—and all I want is a drop of water."

16

I have wasted my life searching for my mother. I exhaust myself and do not find her. And then when I return, I find that my father has started losing himself as well—a loss from which there is no return. What does it matter now whether he killed her and threw her in the well, like a small kitten, or if she left of her own accord, or if she returned to Argentina to search for the life she had left behind there? What does it matter now whether I am the daughter of Malcolm Porter or the daughter of the shaykh?

I had to make a complete circle in order to arrive at this place, the very same place where I began.

Here I am returning; I return to witness the demise of my father, who will never die. But then, "He is dead... he is dead!" my aunt screams from his room.

The blue tent, which the men of the *haara* and the workers pitched the night before, looks from the rooftops of the upper *haara* like an inflated, sky-blue balloon, lifted high by the wind, which pulls tight on the eight thick cords tethering it to the ground. Lined up carefully in the courtyard, the dark-colored straw and wooden chairs peep out from beneath the tent. Women's voices rise up, repeat, and then just as suddenly relent. Their lamentations come and go, rising while the wind pushes against the blue tent, which stretches over their heads like a vast sea. Their voices pour forth from deep inside and rise up as though escorting the wind in all its power. Most of the chairs fill up, while my aunt, who is seated near the corpse's head, scans the crowd with her red eyes, looking at the faces of the seated women and the few empty chairs. The chairs are filled with women who cover their heads with white *mandeel*s and don black dresses reaching their ankles. I turn around and take the small stairs along the wall of the upper *haara* leading up to the narrow terrace. From the very last window of the *haara*, I see Muti'a's darkened room. The wooden shutters are closed over the window that overlooks the courtyard in the *haara* where the old man's corpse is laid out. I uproot my body, which is attached to the iron bars of Muti'a's window, retreat a little bit and look inside again. I can just about see the shadows of furniture and the spacious large bed turned on end in the corner of the room. I see the orange curtain that divides the deserted room into two parts, half for receiving guests and cooking and half for sleeping and washing.

A slow cry, mixed with words, emanates from my father's female relatives as soon as they enter the square. I enter through the black gate and see these women waving their white *mandeel*s at my aunt and my father's first wife. They exchange words over my father's corpse, words only they can hear. My aunt remains in her place near my father's head. She leans her body a little closer to him and mutters, and then just as suddenly reclines to rest against the chair's back. My brother's wife, silent and yellow, sits across from her.

I approach and sit behind my aunt, who has summoned me to the front row, to sit near the corpse. I see her stony face and its skin's darker color. She fixes her eyes on my father's face as though contemplating nothingness. Her eyelashes quiver and her lower lip trembles. I ask myself, what must she be thinking now? Does she think that this is the first time in her life that she'll be able to speak without him shutting her up? She starts talking, asking the woman sitting behind her about her children and her female relatives, whom my aunt hasn't seen in a long time, then smiles. My brother's wife leans her head near to my aunt's and whispers to her... and, her eyes fixed on my father's face, my aunt suddenly tenses the muscles in her own. "All your waiting has finally paid off, Shams," she is no doubt saying to herself, while beating the palm of her hand against her lower thighs. Now that man can no longer shut her up, or yell in her face, or set Ibrahim against her. She holds the shaykh's hand, a cold, rigid, yellow hand. Does she say to herself, "Only now am I able to hold your hand without fear"? To hold your silent, weak, debilitated hand, which I used to need and now is not what it was? Is it my aunt who says this or me?

Your first wife is sitting near you, father, the one who bore you only one son. She is the only one left. I hear her whispering to you. My aunt sits across from her. Sitting around your cold head are two women who loved you, who hated you, who were always near you and always far from you. I don't know what I'm saying. Did I love you? Did I hate you? I searched for you and did not find you— this is enough to make me hate you forever. I see my aunt as her fear leaves her; every time she takes hold of your motionless hand, she has a little less fear. Is there fear here? Is what Muti'a told me true—that there is no such thing as fear, only people who are afraid? Fear trapped my aunt in this place; my mother fled because she feared it. She was afraid of fear. She was afraid that it would inhabit her and keep her stuck in this place like one of the *haara*'s stones.

The men enter, quickly pick up the shaykh's corpse, and take it out. The deathbed is folded in the middle and the courtyard is empty once again.

I am not strong enough to stand. My daughter moves inside me and hurts me. She presses powerfully on my womb. My daughter is pressing on the gates of the world; she wants to come out.

My little daughter Miriyam was born soon afterward. The nurse didn't leave her in the room. She took her the moment she came out of me. I saw her for only a second. I heard her voice all the way from the end of the hospital's long corridor.

The room spins around me and doesn't stop spinning. The ground powerfully pulls my body toward it. I almost fall over but then I find myself holding onto the bed. I pass my hand over my belly. It is cold, tender and delicate. My hand slides as though my skin were melting underneath it and becoming liquid. I press harder and the surface of my belly contracts and sinks into the spot that is suddenly empty.

I return to the *haara* from the hospital and find nothing, a house as empty as my hand. Why do I keep feeling that what I hold in my hands is at the very same time adrift in the wind? I hold it, but cannot hold onto it... It is mine and yet I don't have it. Why at this moment, the moment of return, is there still a lump lodged somewhere between my heart and my mouth? It neither settles nor wishes to leave. Why does happiness pass right above my head and near my skin, but not reside within me? Why don't I feel certain of anything? How far are we from the image of what we want to be?

I return here and find nothing. A house as empty as my hand. I explore impossible things and ignore that what I am searching for inhabits me—it is inside me and I simply must recognize and accept it. I ignore the fact that the past has escaped me and that I cannot let it go. I ignore that what I want is something specific to me; I am trying to find a history that is not like my mother's.

I do not know what my mother entrusted to the priest. My brother says that it was papers regarding her inheritance and renunciation. I do not want to know. I do not want anything. Let them come and take everything. I didn't find what I was searching for outside and I won't find it. It doesn't exist—not in the *haara*, not in the fields, not in its tiled floors, not in its rooms. I'm searching for something I have kept stored away. Why do I go so far and still not see it? It is inside me; why do I close my eyes to it?

I come back simply to experience my father's absence myself. I see her sitting there, my aunt whom I left here, a tree whose roots have dried up and which remains suspended in the dust, bearing no fruits or leaves, a rotten, desiccated, cracked stump. I sit in front of her creating bridges between memories; I connect them to each other like someone sewing together an old dress that must be mended to be worn.

My brother comes back from the city, where he has found work, and then leaves. Every time she comes with him for a visit, Doha takes with her some of the household goods of the *haara*—carpets, then the chandeliers, then the furniture from the summer living room. Doha comes and then leaves… She comes and goes… and on each of her visits, the house is further emptied of its furniture and other contents. "She is never satisfied!" says my aunt, who has put on weight and can no longer do any of the housework. She cuts up green beans to dehydrate them, puts slices of tomatoes and eggplants out in the sun to dry, and prepares to pickle cucumbers in vinegar and salt. She does all of this while sitting on the ground.

Doha replaces the love that my brother doesn't give her with the things that she acquires from the house, including its furniture. She takes things from my aunt, who has become more generous with her suggestions about what she should take. The death of her brother transformed my aunt from a woman who kept the smallest of household trinkets in the cupboards into one who gives away everything she touches. Since his death she has started throwing things away mercilessly. As soon as the men took him out of his bed, she threw it away. She started getting rid of things that she had kept her whole life but never used. I enter the *haara* and hear her asking my brother's wife, "Could you use this?" while holding a big china bowl or plate. "This? ... what about this?"... fabric for curtains, pillowcases, and tables. My brother's wife takes everything. She doesn't know what she'll do with it all, but she justifies taking it, by saying she might need these things some day.

The big tree remaining in the courtyard marks the house, which is now emptied of its people. The walnut tree, which my father always said was the strongest tree, has started to dry up. This started long before I labeled what was happening the Age of Dryness. For years now—it's difficult to be exact—the bark of its trunk has been disintegrating. Its center hollowed out year after year, after which its trunk opened like Ali Baba's cave. I do not know when I first saw the cracked-open, dark inner trunk. Troops of ants start marching along a path up to the top of the trunk and then to the bottom in the dirt, where their villages are spread out at its dark, hollowed-out base... despite all this it is round like a womb, like a child's hiding place. But it is neither a shelter nor a comfort. It was delicate and had no power to protect itself, so how could it protect someone else?

My brother's children carouse freely in the *haara*'s precincts. Their voices mingle with my aunt's shouting and Doha's curses. When they're bored, they climb up to the upper *haara* and knock on the locked doors. The successive echoes of their knocking shake the walls of the rooms, now nearly empty of furniture.

My brother's children grow up, move away and return with new shapes and faces. My aunt struggles to recognize them and remember their names.

My daughter slides off of my lap. I hold her well so that she cannot free herself of my arms. They surround her small body, which is constantly in motion like a shuttle on a loom.

My mother... I mean my daughter slides off my lap, climbing down to toddle on the ground like a colorful bird who has not yet learned how to fly, who wants to fly before its time. I keep an eye on her from my place.

She comes back to grab me by my hand. I stand up and follow her small, overfull footsteps. She goes into the summer living room, the room no one ever enters. She climbs up on the only remaining sofa and gets near the table still in the corner of the room. Her little hand picks up a picture, she looks at it, smiles, puts it down and then leaves. I follow her into the outer courtyard. The cat, stretched out near the threshold of the *liwan*, meows when she sees Miriyam. Then she gets up and runs away. She is afraid that the little girl will grab her by the tail again, as she did this morning.

Notes

2   *haara*: in the context of this novel means a big, old-style Arab house consisting of large, long rooms with high ceilings, each of which is completely independent of the others and opens onto an outside yard.

3   the long *liwan*: a long wide room in the central part of the middle *haara*. It is the heart of the house, from which doors on both sides open into the several rooms of the middle *haara*.

6   *qabaday*: often translated "strongman," this means a tough man who holds a position within his community as someone who protects people.

8   *dawwara*: the circular garden of the house, which almost completely surrounds the three *haara*s.

8   the large *liwan*: a large entrance hall that starts from the second iron gate and is about 10 yards long and 3 yards wide. On both sides of it there are several doors that open onto all of the rooms of the middle *haara*.

8   *'uqqal, kuffiyah, sitra, sirwal*: all items of cloth-
    ing that men wear in the traditional dress style of
    the village, including a head cover and wide
    trousers with extra cloth sewn between the legs.

29 *metteh*: a bitter green herbal tea drunk
    through a straw, imported to the region by
    émigrés returning from South America and
    particularly popular in villages.

33 *mughli*: a rice-based pudding served to breast
    feeding mothers.

43 *majlis*: the gathering place where the Druze
    faithful meet.

45 *kafer/kafera*: an unbeliever or infidel, here
    used to indicate someone who cannot be con-
    sidered a Druze.

46 *mandeel*: the long white covering some Druze
    women wear over their heads and which can
    also cover their neck, shoulders, and chest.

110 *roqiya*: a positive spell used for protection,
    such as when people read or say something
    religious for a person who is ill to help that
    person heal.

Translator's Acknowledgments

I first must extend my gratitude to Iman Humaydan Younes, who was more than generous with her time and open with her suggestions about how to make *Wild Mulberries* into a novel in English. Hilary Plum of Interlink Books is a thoughtful and careful editor whom I also would like to acknowledge warmly. Thanks also to Elise Salem, who first gave me this novel and Nada Saab, who discussed it with me in Lebanon in 2004, both of which prompted me to work on this translation. My students in "Arabic Four" Fall 2005 challenged me to think about the text deeply; thanks to Pascal Abidor, Bassil Mikdadi, Ariana Markowitz, Nora Parr, and Dima Ayoub, the last of whom, along with Nadia Wardeh, also served as my research assistant in this period. A generous grant from the Social Studies and Humanities Research Council of Canada made this translation possible. I would also like to acknowledge the contributions of colleagues and friends Laila Parsons and Rula Jurdi Abisaab. Rula especially gave me a great deal of time in a difficult period when she was very busy, to help me with Arabic questions and discuss the translation, for which I am very grateful. Very sincere thanks also to Alessandro Olsaretti for continued intellectual support and assistance. Finally, I would like to thank my family for their unstinting support, especially Julia Hartman, the one who "makes it happen."

I would like to dedicate this translation to the memory of Adele "Deeda" Jurdi and Mark Gualtieri, a sister and brother gone too soon.

ARABIA BOOKS TITLES

A Certain Woman, Hala El Badry, 978-1-906697-07-5
As Doha Said, Bahaa Taher, 978-1-906697-16-7
B as in Beirut, Iman Humaydan Younes, 978-1-906697-20-4
Being Abbas El Abd, Ahmed Alaidy, 978-1-906697-05-1
Cairo Swan Song, Mekkawi Said, 978-1-906697-18-1
Cell Block Five, Fadhil Al-Azzawi, 78-1-906697-03-7
Cities Without Palms, Tarek Eltayeb, 978-1-906697-12-9
East Winds, West Winds, Mahdi Issa al-Saqr, 978-1-906697-22-8
The Final Bet, Abdelilah Hamdouchi, 978-1-906697-06-8
Gold Dust, Ibrahim al-Koni, 978-1-906697-02-0
In a Fertile Desert, Denys Johnson-Davies (ed), 978-1-906697-13-6
Learning English, Rachid al-Daif, 978-1-906697-21-1
Love in Exile, Bahaa Taher, 978-1-906697-01-3
The Loved Ones, Alia Mamdouh, 978-1-906697-09-9
Memory in the Flesh, Ahlam Mosteghanemi, 978-1-906697-04-4
Murder in the Tower of Happiness, MM Tawfik, 978-1-906697-14-3
Spectres, Radwa Ashour, 978-1-906697-25-9
The Calligrapher's Secret, Rafik Schami, 978-1-906697-30-3
The Dark Side of Love, Rafik Schami, 978-1-906697-24-2
The Scents of Marie-Claire, Habib Selmi, 978-1-906697-23-5
The Secret Life of Saeed the Pessoptimist, Emile Habiby, 978-1-906697-26-6
The Tiller of Waters, Hoda Barakat, 978-1-906697-08-2
The Zafarani Files, Gamal al-Ghitani, 978-1-906697-15-0

Buy from www.arabia-books.com &
the BookHaus, 70 Cadogan Place, London SW1X 9AH